RD053103

Ag

D1349083

BLOOD TRAIL

Greg Bannock raises cattle with his father Pete, until rustlers steal their herd — marking the beginning of bad times for their family. But hiding behind a mask of respectability, there is a renegade at work . . . Assisting deputy sheriff Mack Ketchum, Greg finds himself caught up in a plot to kill the rustler gang boss and has to shoot his way out of trouble, still determined to retrieve his herd. When the gun smoke clears, there is a trail of blood throughout the county.

CORBA SUNMAN

BLOOD TRAIL

Complete and Unabridged

LINFORD
Leicester

First published in Great Britain in 2012 by
Robert Hale Limited
London

First Linford Edition
published 2014
by arrangement with
Robert Hale Limited
London

A catalogue record for this book is available
from the British Library.

ISBN 978–1–4448–1817–8

Published by
F. A. Thorpe (Publishing)
Anstey, Leicestershire

Set by Words & Graphics Ltd.
Anstey, Leicestershire
Printed and bound in Great Britain by
T. J. International Ltd., Padstow, Cornwall

This book is printed on acid-free paper

1

Greg Bannock reined in on the crest above the Tented B cattle ranch in Kansas, which he worked with his father, Pete. The sight of his home from this spot never failed to fill him with pleasure. It was all he had ever known and loved. His gaze took in the neat frame house, the corral and the barn, and then shifted slowly to the lone grave on a knoll beyond the house where his mother lay at rest. His memory caused him to sigh heavily. He spotted his father standing in the doorway of the barn, a pitchfork in his hands, and Greg was reluctant to ride in and tell Pete that he had nothing but bad news. Hugh Backhouse, the banker in Ash Ridge, had turned down their application for a second mortgage on the ranch.

It had been useless explaining to

Backhouse that the recent rustling raid had left them in financial difficulties. The banker had cited the cases of two other local ranchers beset by the same problem, and reiterated that the bank could not loan money without sufficient security — his hands were tied by regulations despite his great sympathy for those luckless ranchers who had suffered loss.

Greg stepped down from his saddle and trailed his reins. The bay began to crop the lush grass. Tall and powerfully built, Greg clenched his raw-knuckled hands as a powerful surge of anger filled him. He pulled his lips tight against his teeth. His blue eyes seemed made of steel as he struggled to control his raging emotion. They had been doing so well until the rustlers struck, and the knowledge that they were not the only ones to suffer did little to assuage his feelings. But Greg's concern was for his father. Pete had not recovered from the death of his wife, stricken by a fever that killed her within a week, and the two months since her sad end had brought trouble building up around them.

He stretched his muscular arms and shrugged his powerful shoulders. Around him was the splendour of the Kansan cow country, almost unnoticed now that he was sorely troubled. But he was tough and hard, a product of his environment and the time in which he lived. He had toiled during the ten years since his schooling ended, asking little and wanting no help from anyone. Indomitable in his outlook, he was ready for any trouble; had trained himself to use a pistol, for a man in these uncertain times had to stand up for himself or go under.

He swung back into his saddle and prepared to go on, his narrowed blue eyes sweeping the surrounding range. His right hand hovered instinctively over the butt of the Colt .45 in its black holster, snug on his right hip. He had taken to carrying the pistol since the rustlers struck, and although he had searched the range in all directions after the cattle steal he had failed to get a line on the unscrupulous thieves. But neither had Mack Ketchum, the deputy sheriff of Ash Ridge, whose immediate superior, Sheriff Matt Pegg, bossed the law in Hickman County and operated out of the town of Hickman seventy miles to the west.

Greg's expression hardened as Ketchum came to mind. He had never cottoned to the deputy, who liked nothing better than to throw his weight around, especially on a Saturday night when Ash Ridge was filled with pleasure-seeking cowpunchers in from the outlying ranches. To Greg's mind, Mack Ketchum was a poor lawman, and the stories of his activities in keeping the punchers under control were unbelievable. So far, Greg had not come up against Ketchum, but he knew he would not knuckle under to bullying if his trail ever crossed that of the big deputy.

He touched spurs to his mount and

went forward down the long slope towards the ranch. Now that he knew for certain there would be no help from the bank he would have to ride out again to search for signs of their missing stock. There was little to do around the ranch with the cattle gone. He dreaded having to tell Pete the facts of the situation, but if he could not regain their stock then they were as good as finished.

The trouble had been growing on the range for some time, culminating in the loss of their herd four nights ago. Greg had followed the tracks of the stolen beeves until they disappeared in the hard ground beyond Coyote Creek. With every avenue of help blocked to them, Greg had no option but to ride over the ground again and look afresh for clues that might have been left by the rustlers.

He was riding along a gully that would take him almost to the fenced yard of the ranch when the faint report of a shot reached his ears. He reined in quickly, jumped down from his saddle, and shinned up the side of the gully until he could see the buildings of the ranch. A string of echoes was fading slowly into the distance. Greg's first thought was for his father, and he climbed out of the gully and ran towards the yard. Then he heard the sound of approaching hoofs and slithered to a halt, his hand dropping to the butt of his gun.

A rider was heading for the yard, holding a drawn rifle in his hands. Greg pulled down the brim of his Stetson to shield his eyes from the glare of the sun and noted that the newcomer was a stranger. Greg dropped to his knees and scrambled forward to the three-rail fence bordering the yard, wanting to remain unseen. The rider entered the yard and jogged through the dust at a trot, holding the muzzle of his rifle ready for action.

Greg drew his pistol as he slithered under the bottom rail of the fence. He rose to his feet as the rider headed towards the house. His movement attracted the rider's attention. Greg saw the man's head jerk around, register his presence, then the rifle swung quickly to cover him. Greg was already pointing his pistol at the newcomer.

'Drop the rifle,' Greg called.

The long gun stopped its sideways movement. The man gazed impassively at Greg, at a disadvantage because Greg had him covered. Silence stretched out between them like an intangible force.

'I told you to drop the rifle,' Greg called.

The man looked sinister in a black shirt and vest, with a black Stetson shading his cold, unblinking dark eyes. He had a hard face and an uncompromising expression.

'Did you fire that shot?' Greg demanded.

The man let go of the rifle and it thudded on the ground. He used both hands to curb his black horse, which cavorted nervously. He had the manner of a man who was on a specific errand but had been surprised by Greg's unexpected appearance.

'Let's try a shot at something a li'l easier,' Greg said. 'Who are you and what are you doing here?'

The man gave the faintest of shrugs. He was tall in the saddle but did not have the look of a cowpuncher. He moistened his lips, then cleared his throat.

'You startled me, I guess,' he said at length. 'I wasn't expecting anyone to pop up out of the brush pointing a gun at me.'

Greg said nothing. He remained motionless, his pistol steady as a rock, its black muzzle pointing steadily at the man's belt. The man grimaced.

'I can understand why you are suspicious of me,' he said. 'I heard that shot, and for a moment I thought it had been fired at me. Then I realized it came from somewhere back of the house. I'm just passing through — was calling in to water my horse. I'm Sim Lant.'

'Get rid of your pistol,' Greg instructed. 'Do it slowly, and don't point the muzzle my way. Then step down and get your hands up shoulder high.'

The man's pistol joined the rifle in the dust. Greg walked forward as the man dismounted and raised his hands.

'That's better.' Greg motioned with his gun. 'Go to the left and around the front corner of the house. We'll take a look out back together.'

The man moved easily and Greg followed him closely, but stayed back out of reach. He was suddenly worried by the thought that his father might be in some kind of trouble in the barn. From back there on the crest, Pete had looked to be busy with the chores. They turned the corner of the house and walked along its side towards the barn, thirty yards back. The barn door was wide open but there was no sign of Pete.

'Hey, Pa,' Greg called. His voice echoed from the doorway of the barn.

'Show yourself. What was that shot I heard?'

A man stepped into the doorway of the barn, holding a pistol in his right hand which was levelled at Greg and Lant. Greg was behind Lant, and not directly covered by the drawn gun. Lant halted abruptly.

'Who's that with you, Lant?' demanded the man in the doorway.

Greg caught his breath. A pulse began beating powerfully in his right temple. He cocked his pistol as he eased to the right to clear Lant, who remained motionless.

'What was the shot I heard?' Greg demanded.

'I shot the old man,' the stranger replied. 'He grabbed for a gun when I faced him.'

Lant half-turned and reached out to grasp Greg's gun. Greg moved to his left, swinging his left fist as he did so. His knuckles smacked against Lant's right temple. Lant fell back, leaving Greg with no cover. The pistol in the stranger's hand shifted its aim slightly, the muzzle looking as big as a cave mouth. Greg fired instinctively, the crash of the shot sending echoes thundering through the barn. He saw dust spurt from the stranger's shirt front. Greg pulled back on his hammer but the stranger was twisting away and slumping to the ground with blood spreading through the thin fabric of his shirt.

The action seemed like a dream to Greg's mind. The stranger landed on his back and was still, his gun gone from his hand. Greg gasped for breath. Gun smoke was thick and pungent in his nostrils. He looked at Lant, saw the man trying to regain his feet, and caught the glint of a pocket gun being pulled. He shifted his aim and fired again. The slug hit Lant in the throat. Lant fell back heavily as Greg ran into the barn to check on his father.

Pete Bannock was lying on his back towards the rear of the barn, his pistol down beside him. Blood was soaking the front of his shirt. He was unconscious and inert, his rugged face deathly pale.

'Pa!' Greg holstered his gun, ran forward, and dropped to his knees beside the older man. Relief surged through him when he discovered that Pete was breathing. He opened the shirt to expose a neat round bullet hole under his father's bottom right rib.

Moving without conscious thought, his senses dulled by shock, Greg straightened and lifted his father gently from the ground. He staggered out of the barn and across to the house. As he crossed the porch the sound of a horse approaching alerted him and he threw a quick glance across his shoulder. Relief stabbed through him when he recognized the deputy, Mack Ketchum, entering the yard at a canter. Sunlight was glinting on the law badge pinned to Ketchum's shirt.

Greg eased his father on to a couch in the big living room and went back to the front door. Ketchum was dismounting. He was a tall man, solid, with plenty of weight, most of it hard muscle in all the right places. His brown eyes were narrowed under the wide brim of his Stetson. He was sweating, and cuffed back his hat to wipe his forehead on a sleeve. He was not a handsome man. His face was angular, his eyes deep set, and his habitual expression suggested an aggressive temperament.

'What's going on, Bannock?' Ketchum demanded. 'I heard shooting as I came in. I saw you carrying your pa into the house — what's wrong with him?'

'He's been shot!' Greg spoke through clenched teeth. 'I need to tend him. Come on into the house.'

'Did you shoot him?' Ketchum asked they entered.

'The hell I did! There are two strangers out in the barn — both dead. One of them shot him — the other tried to shoot me.'

'Jeez!' Ketchum turned and ran from the house. He paused on the porch and looked back at Greg. 'Do what you can for your pa. I'll take a look at the strangers. You stay in the house until I get back.'

Greg fetched a bowl of water and used a cloth to bathe his father's wound. With most of the blood removed the bullet wound did not appear to be too serious. He thought it was close enough to the right lower rib to have missed any vital organs. The bleeding had eased, but it looked as if the bullet was still in the wound. Pete Bannock opened his eyes. His face was ashen, his gaze vacant. He groaned.

'Stay still, Pa,' Greg said soothingly, his voice filled with a tremor. 'How are you feeling?'

'What happened?' Pete Bannock, in his middle fifties, was thin like a bean pole, with no spare flesh on his lean frame. His blue eyes suddenly showed a glint of awareness. 'Say, I remember now. A stranger came into the barn through the back door. He had a gun in his hand and took me by surprise. He plugged me before I could get my gun into action.'

'Don't worry about him, Pa,' Greg said softly. 'He's dead. There was a second stranger coming into the yard, and I took care of him too. Ketchum has just turned up. He's gone out to the barn to look at the strangers.'

'What the hell is going on, Greg?' Pete tried to sit up but groaned and fell back.

'Just stay still, Pa,' Greg said sharply. 'I'll put you in a wagon and take you into town. The doc will have to look at you. I think the slug is still in there.'

'So you killed two men, huh?' Pete closed his eyes. 'All that practising with a gun sure paid off! And I thought you were wasting your time. But who are those men? Why did they ride in here looking for trouble? The one I saw was ready to shoot me on sight. I never set eyes on him before. How'd you make out in town? Is Backhouse gonna lend us dough?'

'No, Pa.' Greg suppressed a sigh. 'He

said he'd like to, but he's bound by rules. If we don't have security then he can't help us.'

'So you'll have to ride out again and look at the sign those rustlers left, huh? Maybe you missed something. If we can get those stolen beeves back then we've still got a chance.'

Greg shook his head. 'You're clutching at straws, Pa,' he said harshly. 'Those steers are long gone and we'll never see hide or hair of them again. They were stolen to ruin us, and we've got to hang on to see who shows up to buy us out.'

'Like those two men in the barn, for instance?' Pete's voice grew fainter as he spoke.

'Yeah, I'd sure like to know where they came from.' Greg heard the sound of a boot outside on the porch and got up to face the door, drawing his gun with a slick movement.

Mack Ketchum peered around the doorpost. He saw the gun in Greg's hand and held up both his hands. 'Hey,

I'm on your side,' he said quickly. 'You did a good job on them two, Bannock. They're both dead. I heard you've been buying lots of cartridges. So you've been practising, huh? Were you expecting trouble?'

'It looks like I did the right thing.' Greg had to make an effort to control his voice. He was trembling inside, and the knowledge that he had killed two men in defence of his own life filled him with an odd sense of horror. 'We've sure got trouble on our stoop,' he said. 'Those two out there are strangers. Pete and me, we haven't seen them before. How about you, Ketchum? Have they been seen around town?'

'I ain't ever set eyes on either of them,' Ketchum said. 'So they came in here and started shooting without warning, huh?'

'I was in town this morning to see Backhouse about a loan,' Greg continued. 'I was coming back up the gully when I heard a shot and climbed up to look at the ranch. I saw a stranger

17

riding into the front yard. He had his rifle out, and looked ready to use it. I got the drop on him and we went round to the barn — I'd seen Pete in the doorway of the barn from the ridge back yonder. The second man came out of the barn with a gun in his hand. He said he had shot Pete, and I took it up from there.'

'So they came here on the prod.' Ketchum nodded, his fleshy lips compressed into a thin line. 'How'd you make out in town? Did you get a loan?'

Greg shook his head. 'No dice. With the stock gone, we've got no security.'

'That's too bad.' Ketchum thrust out his bottom lip and grimaced. 'It looks like you've been set up and cleaned out. Have you had any offers for the spread?'

'No. What makes you ask?'

'I was talking to Tom Gallie a couple of days ago. The same thing happened to him. His herd was run off two weeks ago, and when he tried at the bank for a loan he was turned down. I'll tell you what I told Gallie. There's a land speculator opened up an office in town. He's looking locally for small spreads to buy. It wouldn't hurt for you to have a talk with him. He might be able to steer you in the direction of someone who wants to buy in around here.'

'But we don't want to sell out,' Greg protested.

'Sure you don't, but if Paul Sullivan can tell you who is out to buy range around here you might get a head start on finding out who is back of this rustling. How's your pa?'

'I'm gonna put him in the buckboard and run him into town to see the doc.'

'I'll get your team ready and bring the buckboard round to the porch. You can take in the two corpses while you're at it.'

Greg nodded and returned to his father. The shooting had wrought a change inside him and he was only now becoming aware of it. He had never shot a man before and his mind was alive with shocked speculation. He had often wondered if he would have it in him to fight back if the chips ever went down, and now he knew. He felt impatience tug at him, but fought it off. He had to get Pete to the doctor in town, and then he would make the time to check out that land speculator. After that he would scout the range again, aware that a herd of steers could not just vanish into thin air.

There was a strange air of menace over the ranch as he helped Ketchum load the dead to the back of the buckboard. Greg saw a different side to the deputy. Ketchum seemed ordinary, normal, without the usual swagger that accompanied everything he did in town. He seemed almost human as they lifted Pete into the buckboard and placed him on a pile of straw.

'Where's your horse?' Ketchum demanded.

'Hell, it's still down in the gully,' Greg replied.

'OK. You start driving this rig to town and I'll pick up your nag. I'll catch up with you shortly. And keep your eyes lifting after this. If there are men out here hoping to take over this place then they could be planning to have another crack at you.'

'I'll be ready for them,' Greg said harshly.

He got up on the driving seat and flicked the reins of the team. As the buckboard rattled across the yard Greg glanced around. He was tense inside, his nerves jumpy, and he was watching for trouble as he hit the trail to town. He glanced over his shoulder from time to time, checking on his father. Pete was motionless on a bed of straw, and seemed to be unconscious. Worry tugged at Greg's mind. If anything happened to Pete ... He left the thought unfinished and urged the team on. Ash Ridge seemed to be a whole lot further away than he recalled.

The town was seven miles from the ranch, and Greg felt every bump and hollow in the meandering trail. The buckboard bounced incessantly, and his concern for Pete grew as they continued. When he spotted movement ahead he drew his pistol and held it ready, until he recognized the slight figure riding a grey horse, whom he knew well. Dora Jameson, the daughter of Will Jameson, who owned the general store in town. Greg glanced around, wondering where Ketchum had got to. Dora spotted him and waved.

Greg felt some of his tension dissipate as he acknowledged the wave. He smiled. He had been sweet on Dora for as long as he could remember. His smile faded when he recalled that he had arranged to stop by the store after seeing Backhouse, the banker, but had forgotten to do so after the financial blow he had received. He kept the team moving as Dora came up. She was tall and fair-haired, her eyes blue like cornflowers. Dressed in jeans and a dull-brown denim jacket, she wore a small flat-crowned white Stetson. She was beautiful, with a vivacious manner that showed even though she was in a saddle. She lifted a hand in greeting and reined in, expecting him to halt, but he jerked a thumb to the back of the buckboard and she rode close to peer in.

He saw her expression change as shock filled her, and she signalled him to stop the team. He shook his head and she rode up alongside the driving seat.

'I daren't stop,' he called above the rumble of the wheels on the hard trail. 'I need to get Pete to the doc as soon as I can.'

'What happened?' Dora demanded.

'I'll tell you later.' He urged the team on. 'Follow me back to town.'

She nodded and rode beside the buckboard. Her face was pale with shock. Greg glanced at her, and shook his head when her gaze met his.

'I'm sorry about this morning,' he called. 'I got some bad news from Backhouse. He wouldn't give us a loan. When I came out of the bank I rode straight back to the ranch to talk to Pete about it.'

'Pull up and I'll ride with you,' Dora said loudly.

Greg hauled on his reins and the buckboard lurched to a halt. He looked around while Dora tied her grey to the back of the vehicle, hoping to see Mack Ketchum coming along the trail, but there was no sign of the deputy. Dora climbed into the buckboard and bent over Pete. She looked up at Greg, her expression showing fear.

'I think your pa is dead,' she called. 'Come and look at him, Greg.'

He dropped the reins and climbed quickly over the seat into the back of the wagon, alarmed by her words. As he dropped to his knees beside Pete he heard the crack of a rifle, and a bullet smacked into the woodwork of the buckboard, struck an iron strap, and ricocheted with a dull whine. Dora uttered a cry of fright and dropped flat on the floor of the vehicle. Greg drew his pistol and turned to look over the seat he had just vacated. He saw a puff of gunsmoke drifting away from a knoll about fifty yards ahead. Even as he spotted the smoke a rifle cracked again, and he felt the tug of a bullet that struck his pistol holster. He was untouched by the bullet, and dropped down beside Dora, filled with sudden cold fear.

2

Mack Ketchum rode out of the Bannock yard and headed for the gully where Greg had left his horse. He found cover on the rim of the gully, twisted in his saddle to gaze at the buckboard raising dust along the town trail, and his face pulled into harsh lines as he watched Greg drive the vehicle out of sight. A picture of the two dead men in the back of the buckboard was burned in his mind, as if someone had put it there with a hot branding-iron. The last thing he had expected was Greg Bannock coming out on top in a fight with Sim Lant and his tough sidekick, Bat Johnson. A savage urge of furious emotion gusted through Ketchum and he sweated as he struggled against an impulse to chase after Greg and shoot him down in cold blood.

Damn Sim Lant to hell and gone! Ketchum had warned the gunman to take care in tackling Greg, but Lant, an arrogant desperado, had merely laughed; now he and Johnson were dead. Ketchum shifted uneasily in his saddle. Lant and Johnson had been members of Chad Sewell's rustling gang, with whom Ketchum had ridden until a couple of years back, when he had forsaken the wide-loop trail to take up law-dealing. But Sewell and his rustlers had not permitted him to forget his past and had turned up in Ash Ridge with a deal for him to help them clear the local range of stock — or else.

The gang had started local rustling operations with a raid against Mort Hallam's cattle spread — H7 — the largest ranch in the county, and then they attacked several of the smaller ranches to create confusion. Lant was supposed to have dealt with the Tented B, persuading Pete Bannock into pulling up stakes and quitting, but obviously something had gone wrong and the shooting of Pete together with the attempt to murder Greg, had come unstuck. Greg had upset the apple-cart with his ready gun, and now the plan appeared to be in tatters. However, a third rustler, Grat Bender, was waiting somewhere along the trail to town just in case Lant did something wrong, and if Bender managed to kill the Bannocks then all was not lost.

Ketchum tethered his mount and descended into the gully. Greg's horse was grazing quietly. Ketchum stepped up into the saddle and continued up the gully until he emerged near the corral of the ranch. He transferred to his own horse and continued in the direction of Ash Ridge, leading Greg's mount. When he heard distant shots he grinned and went forward at a lope, hoping that Grat Bender was having more luck than Lant and Johnson.

★ ★ ★

Greg was shocked by the ambush. He pressed a hand to Pete's chest.

'He's still alive, Dora,' he said, 'but he's worse than I thought. Keep your head down and I'll make a run for that knoll where the shots came from. If I don't get Pete to the doc pretty soon he'll die.'

He slid over the back of the buckboard, pistol in hand, then changed his mind about making a run for the knoll. He untied Dora's horse and jumped into the saddle, kicked the animal into motion, and swung wide from the buckboard. He hunched over in the saddle to minimize his target area, the big .45 Colt steady in his right hand, and angled away to the left in a circle to approach the knoll from one side. When he hit rising ground he pulled the horse to a halt and dived from the saddle. The echoes of the two ambush shots had faded and now a deathly silence hung over the range. The sun was glaring down from a brassy sky. Greg sweated as he got to his feet and went forward cautiously.

He found the knoll deserted when he reached it, and turned slowly to observe the reverse slope. He saw a rider heading into thick brush some forty yards away, vanishing before Greg could take note of more than one detail: the horse the man was riding was black with a white left lower hindleg. He holstered his gun and waved to Dora to bring the buckboard to where he was standing, and continued to watch the spot where the unknown rider had disappeared.

Moments later Dora brought the team to a halt at the bottom of the slope and Greg ran down to join her.

'You'd better get on your horse and head back to town alone,' he advised. 'It's not safe to be close to me. I'll see you at the store after I've got Pete looked at. Go on, Dora, get out of here. I need to raise dust.'

She nodded. Her face was pale and fear showed in her blue eyes. 'Please be careful, Greg,' she said as she jumped down from the buckboard. She ran to her horse and mounted, turning once to gaze at him before spurring the animal and heading away to the right. Greg watched her go, his brow furrowed. He was finding it difficult to believe what was happening, but he was resolute and highly alert as he continued towards town.

Ash Ridge, which gave the cow town its name, was sky-lined to the north of the huddle of buildings that fronted either side of the broad single street. It was a purely functional town with few if any amenities, bleak and dusty, and its 400 or so inhabitants were dour, indomitable folk who sweated through the overwhelming heat of the summers and shivered under the blasts of blue northers in the depths of the icy winters.

Greg ran the team along the street and halted at the doctor's office. It was early afternoon and the inhabitants were mostly indoors under cover from the burning sun. He threw down the reins and hurried across the sidewalk to the doctor's door; he tried it, found it was locked, and hammered on the centre panel with a frantic fist. The sounds echoed across the silent street.

'Doc, are you at home?' Greg called. He paused, breathing heavily, and listened intently for sounds within the house. When he heard footsteps approaching the door he heaved a sigh of relief. The door was unlocked and opened. Greg looked into the whiskered face of Doc Henderson, a diminutive man, past middle age, slight of build with pale-blue eyes and a small-featured face that had lost its youthful lines and was almost round in appearance. Henderson had a double chin; his beard was greying, and his hair was slowly turning to the same colour from black.

'Greg,' Henderson observed in a low, pleasant voice. 'What brings you to my door in a sweat? Is it your father?'

'Pete is in the buckboard, Doc,' Greg gasped, wiping his face. 'He's been shot bad, and I think he's dying.'

Doc Henderson moved fast for an older man. He passed Greg and climbed into the buckboard with surprising agility, paused at the sight of two dead men lying in the back of the vehicle, then glanced at Greg but said nothing. He dropped to his knees beside the unconscious Pete Bannock and his experienced hands went to work as he made an initial examination.

'It doesn't look good, Greg,' Henderson commented at length. 'The bullet is still in there, and will have to come out immediately. But Pete is tough, and should beat this if none of his vitals are damaged. Let's get him into my office and I'll see what I can do.'

They carried Pete into the office and put him on an examination couch. Greg stood in the background, watching while Doc Henderson cut the shirt off his father, whose face was set in a pale mask of shock. Henderson picked up a probe, but turned to Greg before beginning to explore the wound.

'You look like you could do with a

good stiff drink, Greg, so why don't you run along to the saloon and fortify yourself? Come back in about thirty minutes and I'll probably have some news for you. There's nothing you can do here.'

Greg nodded and turned instantly to the door. He stepped out into the bright sunlight and paused to look around. The town looked peaceful and quiet, and he could not believe Pete was lying on the doctor's couch waiting to have a slug removed. He heard hoofs along the street and looked up, his right hand dropping to the butt of his holstered gun. Dora was coming along the street at a canter. Greg did not relax. He watched the girl as she came straight to his side.

'How's Pete?' she asked anxiously.

'We shan't know what his chances are until Doc has removed the bullet,' Greg replied. 'Did you have any trouble on your way back to town?'

Dora shook her head. There was an expression on her face that showed she was having trouble accepting what had befallen them.

'I'm going for a drink.' Greg pulled down the brim of his Stetson to cut the probing sun out of his eyes. 'I'll drop in at the store shortly to see you. I wonder where Ketchum has got to? He was going to pick up my horse from the gully in front of the ranch and follow me into town. He must have heard the shots that were fired, so where is he?'

'Do you think he ran into some trouble that was maybe meant for you?' Dora queried.

Greg shrugged and shook his head. 'After my experiences this morning there's no telling what might have happened. I'll wait around to hear what the doc has got to say about Pete, and then ride out to check on Ketchum.'

'You can borrow my horse if you need to,' Dora offered.

'Thanks.' Greg reached up and grasped Dora's hand. 'Something bad is happening on this range, and if nothing is done about it then it will get out of hand.'

'It looks like it has happened already.' Dora turned her horse and headed for the stable. Greg shook his head and walked along the street to the Golden Saddle saloon. He paused at the batwings and turned to survey the silent street. The peacefulness seemed to mock him, and he sighed as he pushed through the batwings. The saloon was empty except for the bartender, Jack Shreeve, who was seated behind the bar on a tall stool. Shreeve's head was nodding and his eyes were closed. He was a dour man and had little in the way of conversation. He seemed to have no interest in life beyond serving the customers who came his way. He was of slight build, seemed quite old, his hair was white at the temples, and he never used two words where one would suffice.

Greg's boots rapped on the wooden floor but Shreeve did not stir until Greg was standing before him. Then he opened his eyes, peered at Greg, and slid off the stool.

'What?' Shreeve demanded with a hand poised over an empty tall glass, aware that Greg drank only beer and that sparingly.

'Whiskey,' Greg replied. 'Hit me with three fingers, Jack. I've had some real bad shocks this morning.'

Shreeve looked more intently at Greg, nodded, for shock was showing plainly in Greg's eyes, then reached for a smaller glass and a whiskey bottle.

'What kind of trouble?' Shreeve demanded, pouring whiskey into the glass. He slid it in front of Greg, who snatched it up and drank half its contents at a gulp. Shreeve grimaced but remained silent.

Greg set down his glass, threw some coins on the bar, and then leaned an elbow on the polished surface. He felt as if he had just completed a week's work in twelve hours. Shreeve watched him intently.

'You heard of anybody else around

here losing stock to rustlers, Jack?'

Shreeve shook his head. Greg regarded him for a moment, then sighed, irritated by the man's reticence. He finished his drink, slammed down the glass, and stalked out of the saloon. A rider was coming along the street and Greg eyed him. The man was a stranger, his head turning left and right as he traversed the dusty street, missing nothing of his surroundings as he approached from Greg's right. Greg glanced along the street, saw Dora walking to the store from the livery barn, and shifted his gaze back to the stranger. The man glanced at him, seemingly without interest, then reached for his holstered pistol in a fast draw.

Greg saw the man's right elbow bend, his gun invisible until the muzzle swung across from his right side. Greg saw the weapon at the last moment and hurled himself to his right, towards the rear of the horse, which forced the rider to swing violently in his saddle in an effort to bring the gun into action. Greg hit the sidewalk on his right shoulder and rolled into the dust of the street. He heard the crash of a shot as he scrambled to his left to enable his right hand to reach for his gun, and he kept his gaze fixed on the rider. The man was reining his horse about for a second shot. Greg palmed his .45 and cocked it; he triggered the weapon twice in quick succession. The gun bucked in his hand and gunsmoke flew. His first shot missed its target but was close enough to throw the rider off his aim. Greg saw his second shot hit the man in the upper chest. The rider sawed on his reins as he was knocked out of his saddle, and the horse went down with him, legs threshing. Dust billowed in the street.

Greg got to his feet, gun cocked and ready. The horse got up and ran along the street. Greg noticed that the animal was black, and its left rear lower leg was white. Shock hit him hard when he realized where he had seen the animal before — leaving the scene of the ambush on the trail to town. This man had ambushed the buckboard!

Greg approached the motionless figure lying in the dust. Disappointment hit him when he found the man was dead for he would have liked some answers to the questions clamouring in his mind. He looked down into a face that was unknown to him, and wondered where the stranger had come from and why he had ambushed the buckboard.

Greg shook his head as he reloaded the empty chambers in his pistol. He was shocked by the incident. He looked around, ready for trouble, and wondered how many more men were at large with an urge to shoot him. He saw townsfolk coming on to the street, attracted by the shooting; he holstered his gun, then eased the weapon, half-expecting that he would have to use it again before the day was out.

Dora was coming along the street. Frank Lind, the town blacksmith emerged from his forge, gripping a shotgun. The big man lumbered at a half-run to where Greg was standing. A man along the street caught the dead man's horse and began to lead it back to where the rider was lying motionless. Gun echoes faded slowly into the distance.

'Hey, Greg, I saw what happened,' Lind said excitedly. He was tall and muscular; his heavy torso was bare to the waist and covered with a thick leather apron tied across his stomach. 'As I stepped into my doorway for a breath of fresh air I saw this guy pull his gun. For a moment I thought he'd got you, but you acted like you was hair-triggered. What was that all about? Who is this guy? Why was he after you?'

'I sure wish I knew,' Greg replied, breathing deeply to steady his jangling nerves. 'There's been hell to pay all morning.' He related the incidents that had occurred, and some of the converging townsmen turned and hurried along the street to where the buckboard was standing after hearing that it contained two dead men.

'Hell, this trouble must have to do with the rustling that's going on around the range,' Lind said. 'John Parker was in town earlier to see Ketchum but that deputy ain't ever around when someone wants him real quick. Parker said his herd was run off last night, and two of his outfit were shot dead when they caught up with cattle-thieves just before dawn. Have you seen Ketchum around?'

'He was at our place this morning.' Greg grimaced. 'I reckoned he should have caught up with us before now. In fact I'm wondering where in hell he's got to.'

'Someone should ride over to Hickman and tell the sheriff what is going on,' opined Charles Dill as he arrived. Dill, the owner of the two-storey hotel, was the town mayor and leader of the town council. 'Ketchum won't be able to do anything about this. You'll need to have Matt Pegg here to handle it.'

'Does anyone know who this man is?' Greg asked.

A dozen men had arrived and were surrounding the body. They gazed in silence at the corpse, and all heads were shaken. Greg felt as if an icy hand was clutching at his heart, and he had no idea what to do next. Dora came pushing through the crowd to stand by his side. Her face was pale and fear showed in her eyes.

'Dora, tell them what happened this morning after you met me on the trail,' Greg said, and listened stonily while the girl described the incident. Charles Dill shook his head. He was tall and thin, smartly dressed in a blue town suit, and wore a flat-crowned plains hat. His grey eyes met Greg's gaze, and he could see great shock in Greg's pale face.

'You'd better check with Doc Henderson how Pete is doing,' Dill said. 'And I think you should stay in town until the sheriff has come in and made an investigation. The stage will be coming through in about an hour. I'll send a message to the sheriff with the driver. When Ketchum returns, he'll need a

43

statement from you, Greg, so you'd better stick around, huh?'

'Sure.' Greg nodded, relieved that someone had made a decision about what he should do. 'I'll get back to the doc's place. What about the two dead men in my buckboard?'

'I'll get Herb Bean to take care of them,' Dill said readily. 'He can keep the bodies at his place until the sheriff gets here. I expect the town council will pay for their funerals. I'll see that your horses are taken care of. You'll find them in the livery barn when you need them again.'

'Thanks.' Greg grasped Dora's hand and they walked along the street in silence until they reached the front door of the mercantile. 'You wait here for me, Dora,' Greg said firmly, and pushed the girl gently across the threshold of the building when she started to disagree. 'It's too dangerous for you to walk with me,' he rebuked.

Will Jameson emerged from the gloomy recesses of the big store. Dora's father was tall and lean, with a rugged face topped by a thick bush of unruly grey hair. A clean white apron covered his slender figure. His blue eyes were filled with a questioning light.

'What's going on, Greg?' Jameson demanded.

'I wish I could tell you, Will, but I'm completely in the dark,' Greg replied. 'I've found nothing but trouble today.'

'I saw you leaving town earlier,' Jameson went on. 'When I heard the shooting a few moments ago someone stuck his head in the door and yelled that you were in a gun fight, and that you had brought two dead men into town in your buckboard. Is that true?'

Greg nodded. 'That's what happened,' he agreed. 'And Pete is at the doc's, shot bad. Dora will tell you all about it. Keep her here, Will, in case there's more shooting. I'm on my way back to Doc's place. I don't know yet if Pete will live.'

He turned away and crossed the

street to the doctor's office. Half a dozen men were standing around the buckboard, peering intently at the two bodies it contained. Greg paused.

'Has anyone seen either of those two men before?' he asked.

Heads were shaken. Greg sighed and turned away, ignoring the questions hurled at him. He entered the doc's house as Henderson appeared in the doorway of his office.

'Good news, Greg,' Henderson said. 'I took the slug out of Pete and I reckon he'll be OK. He'll be on his back for a week at least, but barring complications he'll soon be up and about again. I can keep him here for nursing, if you wish, and I would advise you to, for a few days at least.'

'Sure, Doc, I'll be pleased if you will keep an eye on him. I won't be able to manage him. I've got a lot on my plate right now, and I need to be able to travel fast if I have to.'

'I heard what happened along the street,' Henderson said heavily. 'You've killed another man. What is going on, Greg?'

'I've got no idea! Three strangers showed up today, all with the same intention — to kill me and Pete. It was bad enough losing the herd, but this is something else and I'm going on the warpath. I can't think of any other way to handle it. Some one is out to kill us, and I have to fight back.'

'Where is Ketchum? I notice he's never around when he's needed.' Henderson put a hand on Greg's shoulder.

'I saw him earlier out at the ranch,' Greg said. 'I reckon I can't wait for him to show up. I'm gonna try and backtrack the rider I killed on the street. He's come from somewhere, and if I can pin that down it'll be something.'

'Take my advice and leave the man-hunting to the sheriff,' said Henderson grimly. 'I hope I don't have to start digging slugs out of you, Greg.'

'I've done pretty good so far,' said

47

Greg with a tight smile.

'You were lucky.' Henderson shook his head. 'Just stop and think for a minute about what will happen if and when your luck runs out.'

Greg shrugged. 'I'll have to take my chances,' he opined. 'I want this business settled before Pete gets up and about again, because the first thing he'll do when he's able to is strap on a gun and go out looking for the men causing this trouble. I'll see you later, Doc. I need to be riding out pretty soon.'

'Well, good luck,' Henderson said.

Greg departed, feeling easier in his mind with a decision made. He went back along the street to where Herb Bean, the town undertaker, was loading the dead stranger on to a wheelbarrow. The man's horse was tethered to a nearby hitch rail. Greg paused beside the barrow. Bean was covering the corpse with a blanket.

'Have you searched him yet?' Greg asked.

'Not yet.' Bean was short and fat. He

wheezed when he breathed. His moon face was over-fleshy, had lost its human shape, and his dark eyes were deep set, almost hidden in wrinkles and folds of fat. He was wearing a black suit as befitted his business, and a black derby hat, which was a size too large even for his big head; it was held in place by his big ears. Lank fair hair hung untidily from under the hat. 'It ain't for me to touch the body until I get an OK from the law. Anything you wanta know, ask Ketchum, if you can find him. You can't set eyes on him when you need him in a hurry.'

'I need a horse,' Greg said. 'Ketchum should be bringing mine into town any time. I'll borrow the dead man's horse if I have to leave in the meantime.'

'The horse is no concern of mine.' Bean snickered, exposing yellowed teeth. 'That's unless it has to be buried with the dead man.'

Greg turned away, not amused by the attempted joke. His eyes narrowed when he saw movement along the street, and saw two riders coming into town at a canter. He tensed, dropping his right hand to the butt of his pistol, wondering if more trouble was approaching, but when he recognized Mort Hallam, who owned the big H7 ranch to the north of Tented B, he relaxed. Hallam had always been friendly with the Bannocks, and was known for his honesty and good living. But Hallam, accompanied by his ranch foreman, Cliff Powley, looked anything but friendly as he came to confront Greg. His face was wearing a harsh expression.

'I've been looking for you and Pete,' Hallam called as he reined in. 'Where's your pa? He ain't out at the ranch, so where is he?'

'What's eating you?' Greg countered.

'I'll tell you what's wrong.' Hallam reined in sharply and the prancing hoofs of his big chestnut sent a cloud of dust into the air. 'I found a dozen head of my prime steers penned up in a gully on your range, and you better have a pretty good reason for how they got there.'

Greg frowned. 'Maybe they drifted across the line,' he suggested.

'I said they were penned up.' Hallam's tone was laced with anger. 'Are you trying to tell me they cut poles and barred themselves in after getting into that gully? You'll have to do better than that. I've been losing cattle for weeks, and I ain't been able to find out where they've been going — until now. You're a dirty, lowdown wide-looper, Bannock.'

'I don't cotton to that kind of talk,' Greg said through his clenched teeth. 'I'm telling you we don't know a damn thing about your steers, or how they got penned up on our grass. We've got more than enough trouble of our own right now. We lost our whole damn herd a few days ago. So back off and pull in your horns before I forget who you are and take you up on your fighting talk.'

'Why, you ornery cuss!' Hallam lost his temper completely and sawed on his reins in rage, causing his chestnut to rear. He pulled the animal back under control and dropped his right hand to the butt of his holstered gun. 'Are you gonna try and bluster your way out of this? It'll suit me fine if you wanta fight. You're wearing a gun, so reach for it.'

Greg controlled his temper and heaved a sigh. He had already killed three men in what had become a nightmarish day, and he did not want to become involved in another life-or-death fracas unless it was forced on him.

'Why don't you calm down?' he said in a placating tone. 'Neither of us can win anything by going off half-cocked. Tell me when you lost your steers and I'll tell you where I was at the time. It should be easy to work out who isn't responsible for the steal, even if we can't pin the guilt where it belongs.'

'You're not gonna weasel your way out of this,' cut in Cliff Powley in a clipped tone. 'If the boss won't draw on you then I will. I don't need any more evidence than what I saw out at that gully your side of Gunsight Pass. You lost your herd, and it looks like you started to replenish it with some of our stock. So get to it, you sidewinder, and work your gun.'

Greg opened his mouth to protest but Powley set his hand into motion and drew his pistol. The next instant gun thunder blasted out the silence, and Greg found himself caught up in yet another shoot-out.

3

Mack Ketchum led Greg Bannock's horse along the trail to town. He was in no particular hurry until he heard distant shots echoing across the vastness of the range. He reined in and listened with a grin on his fleshy face. That sounded like Grat Bender doing his job. He touched spurs to his mount and went on at a canter, looking for the Bannock buckboard. Minutes later, when he reached the knoll where the ambush had been staged, he was just in time to see the buckboard vanishing in a cloud of dust along the trail to Ash Ridge. His grin faded when he saw Greg Bannock on the driving seat, whipping the team into a run. A rider was way out to the right, also heading for town, and Ketchum grimaced when he recognized Dora Jameson.

So what was the shooting about?

Ketchum reined into cover. He looked around but there was no sign of any other rider, and he wondered what had happened to Grat Bender. The rustler should have stopped Greg Bannock dead in his tracks. But that hadn't happened, and Bender was not down, so he had not been bested in the ambush.

Ketchum dismounted and walked around the knoll, looking for hoof-prints. He found the spot where a man had lain in wait for some considerable time; a couple of empty 44.40 rifle cartridges verified his reconstruction of the incident. He saw where a horse had stood in cover way down the reverse slope — the animal had grazed for a long time, and when Ketchum noted where it was heading he fetched his horse and followed the tracks until he was certain that the rider — Grat Bender — was heading for Ash Ridge.

So Bender had called off the ambush when he saw Dora Jameson, and Greg

Bannock's murder would have to be handled in town. Ketchum reined in and sat thinking. He did not want to be anywhere near Ash Ridge when Bender finished off Bannock. He had told Chad Sewell that he was against indiscriminate killing, but if Sewell fancied some blood-letting then nothing short of a bullet through his head would stop him.

Ketchum led Greg's horse when he turned away from Ash Ridge. He rode towards the line shack that was situated on Hallam's eastern boundary, beyond Gunsight Pass. The H7 ranch foreman, Cliff Powley, was getting a rake-off from Chad Sewell, and, with Powley's blessing, the rustlers were ensconced in the line shack and safe from detection. Ketchum began to wonder just what he had let himself in for, although he had not had any chance of turning down Sewell's offer of a business deal. Chad Sewell always got what he wanted, and there were more than a dozen graves along his back trail that were occupied by men who had tried to deny him the pleasure of their loyalty.

During his five years of riding with the rustlers Ketchum had got to know Sewell intimately, and considered that he was lucky to have escaped from the rustler gang with his life. It was not until Sewell turned up in Ash Creek to welcome Ketchum back into the fold that the deputy sheriff realized he had been on a long rein for two years and that Sewell was now ready to take advantage of his official position in Hickman County.

Ketchum rode to the Bannock ranch, turned Greg's horse into the corral, and then continued westward, following the line of the range, which rose in gentle sweeps to the ridge that formed the boundary between H7 and the Tented B spread. Gunsight Pass was a V-shaped natural cut in the rocky ridge which gave access to the higher pastures in the county — all under Hallam's brand. He let his horse pick its own way to the pass, his mind busy trying to think up ways of beating Sewell at his own game, but the knowledge that he would surely die if he made a mistake lay uppermost in his mind and he reached no conclusions beyond the one that he should do what Sewell wanted and hope that the rustler would head for other parts without him when his greed was satisfied. The only alternative was to flee the county, and Ketchum had no intention of following that trail.

A small creek watered this reach of Bannock range, and Ketchum permitted his horse to drink before riding into the pass, following a narrow trail that traced the natural fault in the ridge. The ascent became steeper near the western end, and when he eventually emerged on to H7 range he saw Hallam's line shack only yards away, standing like a sentinel on guard. The place looked deserted, but he expected Sewell to be here without making his presence obvious, for the rustler was skilled enough to avoid detection, even by Hallam's outfit.

The shack was deserted, and Ketchum

could see by its condition that it was not in use. He dismounted and tied his horse to a low branch. As he turned to inspect the shack a figure moved into view at the left front corner of the dilapidated building, and afternoon sunlight glinted on a pistol that was in the man's hand.

'Ringo,' Ketchum greeted. 'Where in hell is everybody?'

'We've got a camp back in cover.' Ringo McFitt holstered his pistol and came forward, grinning. He was tall and solid: all muscle and brute strength. He and Ketchum had been saddle pards for a number of years before joining up with Sewell, but they had split up when Ketchum turned to law-dealing. 'We weren't expecting you. What's wrong?'

'There's been trouble,' Ketchum said, 'and I reckoned Sewell should know about it.'

'Don't tell me they've found out about your past and you've been kicked out of town.' McFitt looked around.

'Are you riding alone, Mack?'

'Sure I am. What makes you ask?'

'I thought I heard a hoof hit a rock down there in the pass.'

'You've got better ears than I have.' Ketchum grinned. 'Go and take a look around if you're feeling nervous. I'll talk to Sewell.'

'I'll come with you.' McFitt holstered his gun and Ketchum led his horse as he accompanied the rustler back around the shack.

'So what's the trouble?' McFitt asked.

'Lant and Johnson are dead. They got it at Tented B, trying to put down the two Bannocks. Old Man Bannock is knocking at death's door, but Greg Bannock turned out to be hell on wheels with a gun. He nailed your men and then headed for town with his father in a buckboard. Bender ambushed him on the way, but didn't finish the job. I saw tracks where Bender pulled out. It looked like he was going on to Ash Ridge, so he hasn't given up yet.'

'The hell you say!' McFitt was shocked. 'Heck, I told Sewell I didn't like any part of this job. It's OK rustling stock, but killing ranchers and taking over their spreads is wrong. Why don't you have a word with Sewell about going back to the old-fashioned business of just stealing cows? We were doing all right then.'

'Sewell has become ambitious,' Ketchum remarked, shaking his head. 'And you know you can't talk sense into him.'

'Well, you'd better watch your step, Mack,' McFitt warned, 'or he might put the finger on you. I've noticed how you always rub him up the wrong way. Tell me, do you do it deliberately or is it down to a natural difference of temperaments?'

'I don't like Sewell.' Ketchum scowled. 'He's no great shakes as a gang boss. He gets strange ideas from time to time, and when he does get a bee in his bonnet he never knows when to let up. If he holds a grudge he can't let go. You know that this new idea of his — taking over small ranches — is gonna be his downfall, don't you?'

'Try telling him that.' McFitt shrugged. 'While I ain't scared of him, I ain't stupid enough to make a stand against him. You know how he throws a fit when he's braced.'

'So why don't you quit?' Ketchum looked his pard in the eyes and saw indecision in their brown depths.

'You know what happens to quitters.'

'I left the bunch.'

'You did!' McFitt grinned. 'So what are you doing back here now, huh?'

Ketchum nodded. 'Yeah, it's what they call the line of least resistance. I could have held out when Sewell showed up two years ago, but I'd probably be dead right now. Maybe one of these days I will shoot him but, with Lant and Johnson dead, Sewell is likely to find himself out on a limb after this, anyway.'

Ketchum led his horse around the

shack and McFitt headed for a stand of trees beside a small, meandering stream. Ketchum caught the reek of a campfire and saw a curl of smoke rising above the tree tops. There was a smell of cooking on the breeze.

'There's hardly anyone around at the moment,' McFitt said. 'Sewell sent them out to hit a rancher called Farrant. He always rides with the crew when they make a strike, but he had that land agent out here from Ash Ridge last night and they talked business till gone midnight. I sure don't cotton to Paul Sullivan, but he knows what he's talking about. If you look at a map of this part of the county you'll see that the ranches Sewell hopes to take over form a half-circle around Hallam's H7 spread. I don't know why, but Sewell's got it in for Hallam, and it'll come to a big war when he decides to lock horns with H7.'

'Sewell is loco!' Ketchum grimaced in disgust. 'He couldn't win nohow against H7. Take my tip, Ringo, and get out while the going is good.'

McFitt shrugged and shook his head. 'I ain't running until I've got some more dough in my pocket,' he said. 'Sewell has got mean lately because he's keeping hold of all the dough so he can buy out cow spreads.'

'So that's it!' Ketchum shook his head. 'Sewell is biting off more than he can chew in one mouthful. I reckon we've both got to get out of this before the big blow comes.'

They walked under the trees. Ketchum saw that a camp had been made within their cover. Seven horses were tied to a picket line stretched between two trees, and Ketchum tied his horse there. A guard was walking around the perimeter of the camp. Blanket rolls were spread around a campfire, where a man was busy with pots and pans. Ketchum frowned as he took in the scene — it reminded him too clearly of his days as a rustler. He saw Chad Sewell seated on a tree stump nearby. The rustler boss was cleaning his guns.

Sewell heard their approach and looked up quickly, his hand flitting to the butt of his nearby rifle. He grimaced when he saw Ketchum, and got to his feet with a scowl coming to his harsh face. Chad Sewell was in his late forties, a tall, lean man who looked as tough as old saddle leather. His thin face showed contempt for everyone and everything, as if he hated the world and everything he saw in it. He was dark-haired, and wore an unkempt black beard. His eyes were narrowed; glowing with an inner brilliance that seemed unnatural.

'What the hell are you doing here, Ketchum?' Sewell growled. 'I thought I told you to stick around Ash Ridge. I don't want you wandering around the range. If someone saw you coming in here they might ask awkward questions.'

'I'm only doing my job,' Ketchum replied easily. 'I'm looking for sign of the rustlers that are bothering the county. Haven't seen any around on your travels, have you?'

'Is that supposed to be funny? I don't like funny men, Ketchum, and I don't want you putting any energy into that law job. You carry out my orders; understand?'

'Sure!' Ketchum shrugged. 'I only dropped by to bring you some bad news.' His eyes glinted as he explained about Lant and Johnson.

Sewell heard him out in silence, then began to rage as he walked around the fire. He cursed angrily for several minutes before coming to a halt, his tanned features showing the dull crimson of unreasoning rage.

'So why didn't you step in when things went wrong?' he demanded.

Ketchum shook his head. 'I didn't get to Tented B until it was all over. Lant and Johnson were dead in the barn there when I saw them, but Pete Bannock had been shot.'

'You should have plugged the Bannock boy then and saved Bender the trouble of making a mess of the ambush.'

'It sure looked like he did just that, but from his tracks I reckon he was heading in the direction of the town, so I guess he's still on the job.'

Sewell considered for a moment. 'You'd better head back to town and find out what's going on. If young Bannock is still alive then put him down — the sooner the better. But do it. I want Tented B. You also better check on Pete Bannock; kill him if he ain't dead. Clean it up for me, Ketchum, or you and I will fall out. Have you got that?'

'I'll handle it.' Ketchum turned on his heel and went to the picket line for his horse. He was filled with a growing certainty that he had to get out of this situation he was in, aware that he could no longer afford to be in any future part of Sewell's plans. He untied his mount and swung into the saddle, wondering how he could break the association without getting killed. It came to him that the only way he would rid himself of the rustler boss was if he killed Sewell. He rode out and headed for the pass, wondering if he could put a slug in Sewell and get away with it.

*   *   *

In Ash Ridge Greg saw Cliff Powley swinging into action and set his gun hand in motion. He clawed his pistol from its holster, his thumb pulling back the hammer as the gun muzzle lifted to cover Powley. The H7 ramrod fired hurriedly; his slug put up a spurt of dust beside Greg's left boot. Greg closed his mind to all thought as he concentrated on his gun play. His muzzle lined up on Powley's chest, and he shifted his aim a few inches higher as he triggered the weapon. The Colt .45 blasted and smoked. Powley uttered a cry and jerked backwards in the saddle under the impact of the bullet. He dropped his gun and then lost his balance. As he fell into the street, Mort

Hallam grabbed for his gun, but stopped the action when he found himself looking into Greg's smoking muzzle. Gun echoes reverberated across the street.

'Call it off, Hallam, before someone gets killed,' Greg warned.

Hallam stared into Greg's hard eyes, saw deadly intention in their grim depths, and thrust his gun back into leather. He curbed his uneasy horse and kept both hands on his reins, holding the animal in check.

'Get down and take a look at Powley,' Greg said sharply. 'I aimed high.'

Hallam dismounted slowly and bent over his foreman. Powley was unconscious. He had a bloodstain on his shirt in the region of the left shoulder.

'It looks like he'll live,' Hallam said.

'He's got more luck than the three men I've killed today,' Greg said.

'You've killed three men?'

'That's right, and they were rustlers. So if you've had stock stolen then we should be talking together, not fighting among ourselves. Do you want to push this further or try to talk it through?' Greg did not relax, and his gun was steady in his hand.

'I guess I jumped to conclusions,' Hallam said hesitatingly. 'And I reckon you would have done the same if you'd found some of your stock penned up in a gully on my range.'

'It looks as if that was what you were meant to think,' Greg mused. 'But if the boot was on the other foot I would have come to you asking questions. We lost our whole herd to rustlers four nights ago, so why would we wanta steal a few head of your stock? I was in town this morning, trying to raise a loan at the bank to buy new stock.'

'Did Backhouse agree to lend you?'

'It was no deal.' Greg shook his head. His earlier visit to Ash Ridge now seemed remote. 'I'm gonna head back to Tented B, check the rustler tracks again, and see if I can't run them down. Our cows didn't suddenly grow wings and fly off this range. I reckon they are being hidden somewhere, and I sure as hell intend to find them. I can't let this rest. We're finished if we don't get our stock back.'

Doc Henderson appeared along the street, carrying his medical bag. He came at a half-run to where Greg was standing.

'Is the shooting over?' Henderson demanded.

'It's done,' Hallam said. 'I went off half-cocked, it looks like. Bannock, if I have made a mistake then I'm sure as hell sorry.'

'Tell Powley how sorry you are,' Greg said.

'I'll bawl him out for jumping into my fight,' Hallam replied. 'When you get around to looking for the rustlers then call in at H7 and I'll send some of my outfit along with you. I've got an interest in their capture.'

'It would be better if you checked around my gully where your beeves are penned and see if you can come up with the tracks of the rustlers. I've got to stick around town until Ketchum gets back, whenever that might be.'

Hallam looked into Greg's eyes for several moments, then nodded his head.

'Sure,' he agreed, 'I guess that'll be the better way to handle it.'

'Pete is at the doc's,' Greg went on. 'He was shot this morning.'

Hallam was shocked, and his face proclaimed the fact. He looked at Henderson as the doctor got to his feet.

'That's right,' Henderson said. 'Greg found two strangers at Tented B when he returned there this morning, and one of them shot Pete.'

Greg listened to Henderson explaining the incident, his eyes studying the street, aware that he had been watching his surroundings intently without realizing it. But he understood that this was how it would have to be from now on. He could not afford to take chances, for he had no idea who was against him.

'I'll talk to you again later,' Greg said. 'There are things I need to do around town, and I want to be ready to ride out as soon as Ketchum shows up.'

Greg turned and went back along the street. Dora was standing outside the store with her father, and he would have kept going when he reached them if Dora had not grasped his arm and halted him.

'Greg, what was that all about with Hallam?' she demanded.

'You shot Powley,' Will Jameson observed.

'I'll tell you about it later,' Greg replied. 'There's someone I need to talk to right now, and it won't keep. I'll come back to you shortly, and if Ketchum shows up in town before I return then tell him I'm waiting for him.'

'You ain't planning on shooting Ketchum, are you, Greg?' Jameson demanded.

'Not at the moment,' Greg retorted.

He went on along the sidewalk to an office on the far side of the saloon which had a large sign outside on the wall beside the door on which the words LAND AGENT were starkly daubed in black paint. A small man, slightly built and wearing a brown town suit, was standing in the doorway. His face was pale, as if it was unaccustomed to sunlight, and he took one step backwards into the office as Greg approached him. His brown eyes were fixed on Greg's intent features like a jack rabbit confronted by a rattlesnake.

'Paul Sullivan?' Greg demanded.

'That's me!' Sullivan replied in a low tone. 'Who wants to know?'

'I'm Greg Bannock. Mack Ketchum told me to come and talk to you.'

'Mack Ketchum? Why would he send you to me? And you're Bannock?' He repeated the name as if it burned his lips. 'Say, what do you want with me?'

Greg was watching Sullivan's face, and saw a momentary spark of fear come into the little man's eyes. The expression was gone in an instant, and so quickly that Greg wondered whether he had imagined it. He had never set eyes on Sullivan before. He felt a quickening of interest invade his mind, and a stab of suspicion followed it because, for a moment, Sullivan had looked like a man with a guilty secret.

'My pa and me, we own the Tented B, in case you aren't aware of the fact, and we lost our entire herd to rustlers four nights ago,' Greg explained.

'So why come to me?' Sullivan demanded. 'Do you think I know where your cows have gone? I can't help you, Bannock, and I've got nothing to say to you. If you'll excuse me, I'll get back to my work. I'm way behind at the moment and I have a lot of catching up to do.'

Before Greg could reply, Sullivan stepped back and slammed the street door. The sound of a bar being dropped on the inside came to Greg's ears, and he stared at the closed door in amazement. Then anger replaced his shock and he hammered on the door.

'Hey, Sullivan, open up, will you? I need to talk to you.'

'I told you I'm busy,' Sullivan called through the door panel. 'Get away from there or I'll complain about you to the law.'

Greg considered Sullivan's attitude and didn't like the suspicion that flickered to life in his mind. He stepped back a pace, raised his right leg, and kicked the door with all the force he could muster. The bar on the inside of the door gave way and the door flew inward, striking Sullivan's face before slamming against the wall and rebounding. Greg's right foot came down on the inside of the threshold, and he hunched his shoulder to catch the door, which struck him and then flew open again. Greg stepped into the office. Sullivan was hunching over, with both hands to his face and blood trickling between his splayed fingers.

'What the hell are you so skittish about?' Greg demanded. 'I need to talk to you, Sullivan, and you're gonna hear me out.'

Sullivan reached into a pocket and produced a handkerchief, which he pressed to his bloody nose. He peered at Greg over the handkerchief, his eyes half-closed, filled with uncertainty. He leaned back against the wall, and Greg had the feeling that the little man would flee at the first opportunity.

'What are you scared about?' Greg demanded. 'I ain't gonna eat you. All I wanta do is ask you a couple of questions.'

'What do you want to know?' Sullivan's voice was muffled by the handkerchief. 'Make it quick. I want to see the doctor — I think you've broken my nose.'

'I never laid a hand on you,' Greg retorted. 'You've just set up in business around here, and I need to know if you've had any would-be buyers enquiring about small ranches that might be offered for sale in the county — particularly Tented B.'

'Why should that interest you? Are you thinking of selling out?'

'No, but I'm thinking that someone stole our herd to force us to think about selling.'

'I can't help you! There have been no enquiries for land around here.' Sullivan edged towards the door and Greg stepped forward and barred his way.

'Stand still while I'm talking to you,' Greg said harshly. 'Has any local rancher put his spread up for sale recently?'

'I haven't had one client making enquiries either to buy or sell. Now let me get out of here.'

Greg suppressed a sigh. He gazed at Sullivan for several tense moments, wondering at the land agent's manner. He reached out, grasped the front of Sullivan's jacket, and almost lifted the diminutive man off his feet. Sullivan squealed like a stuck pig.

'If I find that you're lying to me I'll come back and take you apart,' Greg threatened.

'What are you accusing me of?' Sullivan squirmed helplessly in Greg's grasp. 'You can't come in here and take that attitude with me. I'm a businessman, and I know nothing about rustlers. I'll ride over to Hickman and talk to the sheriff about you. You're nothing but a roughneck and a bully.'

Greg could see that he would get nowhere with Sullivan, and released him. Sullivan fell back against the wall, still holding the handkerchief to his nose. Greg departed, sensing that whatever came up in this grim business, he was certain that he had not finished with the land agent. He paused on the boardwalk and looked around the main street, wondering what to do next. He needed to be riding out to check on the rustlers, but he wanted also to see Mack Ketchum.

He glanced back over his shoulder when he heard a noise from Sullivan's doorway, and dived to his left when he saw the land agent emerging from his office with a small pocket gun in his hand. The gun crashed even as he became aware of the danger. Greg went down on his left side, his right hand clawing for his Colt, and, once again, gun fire shattered the uneasy silence of the little cow town.

4

Chad Sewell felt uneasy. He had a nervous itch between his shoulder blades as he watched Mack Ketchum ride down the pass towards Tented B range; impulsively he drew his right-hand Colt and aimed at Ketchum's unsuspecting back. The temptation to split Ketchum's spine was overpowering but he stifled it and lowered the weapon — Ketchum was still of some use to him. He watched the deputy disappear into the distance and turned away to find Ringo McFitt standing behind him, holding a rifle as if ready to use it.

'What are you up to?' Sewell demanded sourly.

'I got the feeling you were thinking of shooting Ketchum,' McFitt said mildly.

'And what were you gonna do about it if I had?'

'Me?' McFitt grinned and placed the butt of his rifle in the dust and leaned an elbow on the muzzle. 'It ain't none of my business, boss.'

'You and Ketchum were buddies one time,' Sewell mused. 'How d'you feel about him these days?'

'I got no feelings either way.' McFitt shrugged. 'Ketchum and me, we went our separate ways a long time ago. He quit us, and I've wondered why you let him get away with that. Benny Howard wasn't so lucky. When he tried to walk, you shot him in the back. So what was special about Ketchum? How come you didn't cut him down?'

'I knew what he was planning, and I let him go because I thought he could be useful to us later. And he's proved it! We've got things on this range moving along nicely.'

'You know I don't cotton to this business of taking over cow spreads.' McFitt's voice was harsh. 'I reckon you're biting off more than you can chew, boss, and we'll pay heavily for any mistakes you make.'

'I ain't made a mistake in twenty years.' Sewell took a bag of Bull Durham from his breast pocket and built himself a smoke. He scratched a match on the butt of a holstered gun and lit the cigarette. 'And I don't intend to start going wrong now,' he added through a cloud of exhaled smoke. 'That's why I reckon you should ride out now and put a slug in Ketchum. I didn't like the expression in his eyes when he left here. I got the feeling he's planning something that will see me dead or behind bars.'

'Why didn't you shoot him when he was here?'

Sewell grinned evilly. 'I want you to do it, that's why. I need you to prove that you don't give a damn about Ketchum.'

'Hell,' McFitt protested, 'I'm resting my bronc right now — it's got a sore leg. Why don't you send Harmon? He'd shoot his own mother for a couple of dollars.'

'Because I want you to do it,' Sewell snarled like a ravenous cur, 'so quit arguing and hit the trail. If I sent Harmon he'd head straight for the nearest saloon in town and get likkered up. If you ride fast you could catch Ketchum before he hits town. When you kill him, put him where he won't be found — under a cut bank in a dry wash, and then drop it on him. Now get going, and head back here soon as you get the job done.'

McFitt started to protest but realized it would be useless. He clenched his teeth. He recalled what Ketchum had said about needing to kill Sewell, and realized that if he wanted to break with the gang the opportunity to do so was being handed to him on a plate.

'OK,' he agreed. 'I'll saddle up.'

McFitt prepared his horse for travel and rode out. He did not look back, but could feel Sewell's hard gaze boring into his back and he felt uneasy, wondering if he was about to get a bullet in the spine. Then he rounded a bend in the pass and was lost to Sewell's eyes. He rode down to Tented B range and hit a gallop, hoping that what Ketchum had said about disposing of Sewell was not just so much hot air. If they got together and killed the rustler gang-boss they might be able to assume control of the gang and cut out the business of taking over local ranches. They could make a lot of money just by rustling H7 stock.

He reached Tented B, which looked deserted and saw Ketchum's horse tied to the porch rail of the house. He rode in noisily to herald his arrival, and called a greeting as he crossed the yard. Ketchum emerged from the house, chewing on something he had found in the Bannock kitchen, and leaned a thick shoulder against a porch post. His inscrutable gaze was unblinking, his right hand close to the butt of his holstered .45.

'What gives, Ringo?' Ketchum demanded.

'Sewell told me to ride.' McFitt grinned.

'Where are you headed? If you're going into town we can travel together. Come on in and have a bite to eat. Pete Bannock and his son are in town.'

McFitt dismounted and tied his horse to the porch rail.

'What orders did Sewell give you?' Ketchum enquired.

'He told me to catch you before you hit town and put out your light, then bury you under a cut bank. How'd you fancy that, Mack?'

'Are you on the level?' Ketchum looked faintly surprised.

'Would I lie about a thing like that?' Ringo laughed. 'I guess Sewell reckons your usefulness is over.'

'But you're here, Ringo, and you don't look like you're ready to obey Sewell. So what's on your mind?'

'I reckoned it's the perfect way out for me. We get together, kill Sewell, take over the bunch, and make big dough. How does that sound, pard?'

'Better than Sewell's plan.' Ketchum nodded. 'Come on in and let's talk it over. Since I left you back there I've thought up a way of getting rid of Sewell with none of the risks.'

'Do tell!' McFitt grinned as he followed Ketchum into the ranch house.

*   *   *

Greg moved fast when he caught a glimpse of Sullivan's hideout gun lifting for a shot. He dived to his left while reaching for his pistol, and the weapon pulled clear of its holster as Sullivan triggered a hurried shot. Gun fire blasted the heavy silence. Greg felt a pain like a red-hot branding-iron slash across his left forearm but ignored it, concentrating on his gun. He fired when the blade of his foresight lined up on the land agent's right shoulder. The half-inch slug of lead struck home and hurled Sullivan's diminutive figure back in the doorway of the office. Sullivan fell against the doorpost, yelled as he lost his grip on his gun, and then twisted and fell on his face on the threshold.

Sullivan twisted on the floor, groaning in pain, and looked around for his gun. He saw it just out of arm's length, began to reach for it, and then looked up to see Greg on one knee, covering him with a pistol that looked like a small cannon.

'Touch that gun and I'll plug you dead centre,' Greg advised.

Sullivan froze, his face taking on an expression of desperation. He skittered along the floor to the nearest wall and sat hunched on the floor; his left hand pressed against the spreading bloodstain on his right shoulder.

'What I wanta know,' said Greg, getting to his feet, 'is why you shied like a loco horse soon as you set eyes on me. You looked like a man with an almighty guilty conscience, Sullivan, and all I wanted was an answer to a simple question. You've got a lot on your mind, mister, and you better start telling me all about it.'

'How did you expect me to act?' Sullivan's teeth were chattering. 'You bullied me and put me in fear of my life. I thought you were going to kill me. I know you're a killer. I saw you shoot down Grat Bender along the street, and I thought I was next on your list.'

'You know the name of that guy I killed?' Greg demanded. He holstered his gun, grasped Sullivan's jacket, hauled the little man to his feet and dragged him out of the office to the sidewalk. Sullivan moaned in pain and struggled ineffectually, pulling against Greg's hold. Greg slapped him across the mouth. Sullivan yelled even louder, and blood dribbled from a cut on his bottom lip.

'My pa was nearly killed by two hardcases at our place this morning,' Greg said harshly, 'I killed them. A third gunnie ambushed my buckboard when I was bringing my pa in to see the doctor, but he pulled out when I made it too hot for him. I noticed his black horse had a white left hindleg: That guy

89

you saw me shoot along the street was riding a horse that colour, and he started the shooting. Nobody around town knows who he was, but you've put a name to him. He's called Grat Bender, huh? So tell me some more about him. How do you know his name?'

'I don't know anything about him,' Sullivan said quickly. 'I heard some men talking along the street, and Bender's name was mentioned. I don't know any killers. Let me see the doctor before I bleed to death. I'll talk to the sheriff when I can get around to it, and we'll see what he thinks about the way you've handled me.'

'Don't worry, I'll be talking to the sheriff,' Greg retorted. 'Go on, get out of here, you weasel, and you better not let me set eyes on you again while I'm in town. I haven't finished with you yet, not by a long rope.'

Sullivan scurried along the board-walk, heading for the doctor's office. Greg watched him for a few moments, his mind turning over the incident as he tried to analyse Sullivan's attitude. He checked his left forearm. Sullivan's bullet had broken the skin from wrist to elbow, leaving a burn on the browned flesh, but there was little blood, and he was aware that he had been extremely lucky. He went along the street to the doctor's house, wanting to see his father. Sullivan had already scurried into the medical office like a hungry pack-rat.

Greg entered Henderson's house. He could hear Sullivan's voice raised in a whine, complaining at the way he had been treated. Greg went to the door of the office and peered into the room. Sullivan was lying on an examination couch with Henderson bending over him, making an initial examination.

'Doc, how is Pete?' Greg asked.

Henderson looked up at him, then left Sullivan and came to the door.

'He's sleeping, Greg, so don't disturb him. Come and see him in the morning. Are you gonna stay in town?'

'I need to talk to Ketchum, but he ain't showed up yet. I reckon I'd better get back to the ranch. There's no telling what will happen out there with no one to guard the place. Yeah, I'll come back tomorrow. If you do see Ketchum in the meantime perhaps you'll tell him I'll be around later.'

'I'll do that.' Henderson turned away but Greg caught his arm.

'How was Cliff Powley, Doc? Was he badly hurt?'

'He wasn't feeling too good with a .45 slug in his shoulder, but I dug it out and he'll get over it. Why did he tangle with you, Greg?'

'I'm wondering about that, Doc. He came into town with Hallam, who said he'd found some of his steers penned in a gully on Tented B range. I told them I didn't know anything about that, and it developed into gun play.'

'So who put H7 steers on your range?'

'That's what I've got to find out.' Greg grimaced. 'I'll look in to it later.'

'Watch your step,' Henderson warned. 'Someone is sure out to get you and Pete.'

Greg departed and walked along the street to the general store. Inside, he found Dora and her father. Dora was sweeping the floor. Will Jameson was serving a customer. Dora looked up at Greg's entrance, saw blood on his left sleeve, and came running to his side.

'I heard the shooting, but I didn't know you were involved, Greg,' she said breathlessly. 'Are you hurt badly?'

'It's only a scratch,' he replied. 'I'm heading back to the spread, and I want some cartridges for my pistol and rifle. I don't know what is going on around here, but I'm knee-deep in killers who are out to get me. I'm hoping it will be quieter at the ranch.'

'Shouldn't you stay in town until Ketchum gets back?'

Greg shook his head. 'He should have caught up with me long before now, so I'm wondering if something has happened to him. I'll have a look around for him when I get clear of town.'

Dora went behind the counter and fetched Greg two boxes of cartridges.

'Can I pay for these later?' he demanded, and she nodded. He opened the box containing .45 calibre shells and filled the empty loops on his gunbelt.

'Be careful, Greg,' Dora said worriedly. 'I shan't have a moment's peace, knowing you're out there alone.'

'I should be quite safe,' he replied. 'There's nothing out there for anyone to steal. I'll be back early in the morning, and I'll see you then, Dora. So long, honey!'

He left and went along the street to where Bender's horse was tethered. He put his boxes of cartridges into a saddle-bag, swung into the saddle, and sat for a moment, looking around the street. The town was quiet. His left arm was aching but he ignored the discomfort for he had more important things to think about. He had killed three men, wounded Sullivan, and Pete was lying badly hurt in the doctor's house. He had no way of knowing what would happen next, but he had an idea that the shooting was not over by a long rope, and, whoever was behind the trouble, they were all aiming at him.

His eyes took on a chill expression as he considered, and his lips firmed into a thin line when he spotted Mort Hallam entering Sullivan's office. The H7 rancher found the office deserted and emerged to stand looking around the street. Greg wondered what kind of business Hallam had with the land agent, then dismissed the thought from his mind.

Greg rode out of town and hit the trail to Tented B. He was wary as he rode, for he had found nothing but trouble since leaving the ranch that morning, and could not recognize an enemy even if he saw one. He watched for signs of Ketchum, and wondered just where the deputy had got to. The afternoon was wearing away, and he began to fear that Ketchum had found some trouble on the trail.

He reached a stand of cottonwoods by a stream and paused to permit the horse to drink its fill. As he moved on afterwards he heard the sound of hoofs close by and dropped his hand to his gun butt. Two riders appeared, coming from the direction of Tented B, and Greg saw at once that they were strangers. He started to pull his gun in readiness, and a harsh voice spoke to him from behind a nearby tree.

'Drop the gun, mister. I got you covered.'

Greg froze his movement and then took his hand from his gun butt. He raised his hands, controlling the horse with his knees. The two riders came up, grinning. Both were holding drawn pistols. A third stranger stepped out from behind a tree, holding a rifle.

'OK, mister,' the rifleman said. 'Tell us what you're doing on Grat Bender's horse.'

'Where is Grat,' another demanded.

'I don't know Grat Bender,' Greg replied.

'We know what his horse looks like, so how come you're riding it?' the third stranger asked. 'And don't tell me you won it in a card game because Bender never played a card in his life.'

Greg moistened his lips. These three looked like hardcases. He could think of no other reason why they would hold him up, and they were obviously friends of the dead Grat Bender.

'There was trouble in Ash Ridge around noon,' Greg said, thinking fast. 'The man who came into town riding this horse got into a gun fight and was killed. My horse was standing outside the saloon and stopped a stray slug. The town mayor said I could use this horse, and I'll be taking it back to town tomorrow, when the deputy gets back from a trip.'

'Who are you?' asked the man with the rifle.

'I'm Greg Bannock. My pa and me, we own the Tented B ranch.'

'Have you seen any other strangers on this range today?'

'No.' Greg shook his head.

'I think you're lying,' said another of the men. 'I reckon we should take him to see Sewell — he'll soon get at the truth. Bender wouldn't have gone into town today. Sewell warned everybody to stay well clear of the place.'

'So you're Greg Bannock!' The man with the rifle shook his head. 'Hey, fellers, we cleaned out Tented B a few nights ago, and Sewell sent Lant and Johnson in there today to kill the Bannocks. I heard them talking about it last night. So what's happened to Lant and Johnson? What you got to say about that, Bannock?'

'Nothing,' Greg replied. 'I don't know who you're talking about.'

'Where's your pa, then? Lant was supposed to kill him this morning.'

'I haven't been back to the ranch yet,' Greg said readily. 'I've been in town all day.'

'What were you doing in town?'

'I went to the bank to raise a loan.'

'So did you get one?'

'No. I was turned down.'

'We better take a look at Tented B,' said one of the others. 'Perhaps something has happened to Lant and Johnson. Sewell has got us jumping in all directions these days, and I don't know what most of it is about. We'd better do some checking. Sewell will jump on us if we don't get some answers.'

'OK,' said the man with the rifle. 'You heard Varney, Bannock. Head for your spread and we'll check it out. You better be telling the truth, or else. Take his gun, Varney, and mind you don't shoot yourself with it.'

Greg was disarmed, and they set out on the last mile to the ranch.

★   ★   ★

At Tented B, after a meal, Ketchum and McFitt left the ranch and headed for Ash Creek. They rode alertly, ready for anything that might crop up in a world that was hostile to lawmen and rustlers.

'So we're agreed on killing Sewell and taking over the gang, huh?' McFitt said as they loped along the trail.

'We're all heading for disaster if we follow the trail Sewell has picked out for us,' Ketchum surmised.

'But you said you had an idea how to get rid of him,' McFitt persisted. 'How about letting me in on that?'

'The Tented B is run by father and son, the Bannocks. Greg Bannock has turned out to be hot stuff with a gun, and he saw off Lant and Johnson with no trouble. His father was shot and Greg took him into town in a buckboard. I found Bender's tracks after I heard shots being fired at the buckboard, and arrived on the scene in time to see the buckboard going on to town. Bender's tracks were heading in the same direction, following the buckboard at a distance. Bender had orders to take care of the Bannocks if Lant and Johnson made a hash of it. I reckon Bender ain't good enough to stop Greg Bannock, so we'll head for town and find out. If Bannock is still alive I'll tell him where he can find Sewell, and we'll tag along on his trail to see what kind of a job he can make of killing Sewell. If he can't manage it then we'll step in and finish it.'

McFitt grimaced. 'I'd rather do the job myself,' he said. 'If we're not gonna take over those ranches then we don't have to kill the Bannocks. We've already got their cattle.'

'How many men are in Sewell's gang?' Ketchum demanded.

'Fifteen at the last count, I reckon. What that got to do with it?'

'You've dropped out and Lant and Johnson are dead. That leaves twelve, and maybe Bender is done for too. If we go for Sewell and the rest of the gang don't want to be taken over then we'll find ourselves in a war that we won't see the end of. I reckon to set Greg Bannock on Sewell. That will bring down the odds considerable, even if

Bannock doesn't kill Sewell. So let's do it my way, Ringo.'

'Sure. Give it a try. What have we got to lose?'

Ketchum nodded and they continued. Ketchum was slightly ahead of McFitt as they topped a rise, and Ketchum immediately uttered a curse, swung his horse, and dashed back off the skyline. McFitt followed quickly.

'Did you see those four riders coming this way?' Ketchum demanded when he was below the skyline. He pulled his Winchester from its saddle boot.

'I saw them but I didn't get a good look at them,' McFitt replied.

'I recognized Greg Bannock.' Ketchum grinned wolfishly. 'One of the other three is Hank Varney. Take a look, Ringo, and see who the others are. It looks like Bannock has fallen among thieves.'

McFitt dismounted, dropped to the ground and bellied up to the crest. He removed his Stetson before risking a peep over the skyline before easing back quickly.

'Heck, that's Fenton and Sadler with Varney,' McFitt said.

'So what are they doing here, and riding with Bannock?'

McFitt shrugged. 'They're following Sewell's orders, no doubt. What are we gonna do about them? Varney thinks the sun shines out of Sewell's eyes, so he won't join us in a break from the boss, and Fenton will do anything Varney tells him. We'd better play the cards as they fall, Mack.'

'It could turn nasty,' Ketchum warned. 'And I don't want Bannock to know I'm lined up with the rustlers. You better follow my lead. I'm a deputy, and those three with Bannock are rustlers, so I'll try and take them, and you start shooting if it looks like I've bitten off more than I can chew. As from now you're an under-deputy, OK?'

'Sure. Do you want me to stay back here and cover you with my rifle?'

'That sounds about right. I'll keep to their left and give you a clear sight of them.'

McFitt nodded. Ketchum drew his pistol and checked it, then rode over the crest and headed for the riders approaching him. The three rustlers halted immediately and reached for their guns. Ketchum knew what he had to do, and drew his pistol. He was fast on the draw and started shooting without warning, blasting the rustlers. His first shot hit Varney in the chest and he shifted his aim quickly to send a bullet through Sadler's head. Then McFitt's rifle cracked and Fenton lurched sideways out of his saddle.

Greg sat motionless, curbing his horse as it cavorted uneasily. He had recognized Ketchum in the instant before the deputy started shooting, and watched Ketchum coming forward with a big grin on his face, his smoking gun tilted skywards.

'Where did you come from?' Greg demanded. 'I've been hanging around town waiting for you to show up.'

'It's a long story,' Ketchum replied.

'Let me check those guys before we talk.'

Greg dismounted and watched Ketchum look over the downed rustlers. He went forward, took his pistol from Varney's waistband, and slid it back into his holster. Ketchum straightened from his examination.

'I found tracks when I went to pick up your horse in the gully,' he said. 'I followed them, and I think I know where the rustlers are holed up. I was on my way back to town for a posse when I saw you with these three. I noticed that you were unarmed, so I guessed these guys were holding you against your will. That told me they were wrong 'uns.'

'Who was using the rifle back on the crest?' Greg asked, looking up the slope. He saw McFitt coming into view, leading his horse.

'That's Ringo McFitt, an old friend of mine,' Ketchum said. 'He's a good man with a gun and I've taken him on as an under-deputy while this rustler trouble lasts.'

'They said they were taking me to see a man named Sewell,' Greg said. 'From the way they spoke, I reckoned they were rustlers.'

'Well, I recognize one of them as such,' Ketchum said, 'so there ain't much doubt about what they're doing on this range.'

'It's a pity we didn't capture one of them to make him talk,' Greg said, shaking his head. 'I need to get our herd back. We're finished if I don't. We'll have to sell up and shake the dust of this range off our boots.'

McFitt came up, grinning. 'That was good shooting, Mack,' he said.

'This is Ringo McFitt,' Ketchum said to Greg. 'Meet Greg Bannock, Ringo. He and his pa own Tented B. They lost their herd to rustlers a few nights ago.'

'Howdy, Bannock,' Ringo greeted. 'You looked like you were in a pretty tight spot a moment ago. It's a good thing we showed up when we did.'

'I appreciate it,' Greg said. He went on to explain to Ketchum what had occurred on the trail to Ash Creek, and his confrontation with Grat Bender.

Ketchum exchanged a glance with McFitt. 'It looks like Bannock has been doing our job for us, Ringo. Maybe we'd better pin a badge on his chest. That guy you shot in town — Grat Bender, you called him. How do you know his name, if you killed him outright?'

'I was coming to that.' Greg spoke of his meeting with Paul Sullivan, the land agent.

Ketchum listened impassively, without comment.

'And there's something else,' Greg continued. 'Mort Hallam rode into town with Cliff Powley. Hallam said he found some of his stock penned up in a gully on our range, and accused me of doing it. Powley threw down on me, and I had to shoot him in the shoulder.'

'You sure as hell have been busy,' Ketchum replied. 'So Sullivan acted suspicious when you spoke to him, and you roughed him up.'

'You think I was wrong to take him on?' Greg asked.

'Hell, no! I had doubts about him from the minute I laid eyes on him. But I reckon he's of no account; a bullet hole in his shoulder should hold him for a spell. We'll get around to him later.'

'So where are the rustlers holed up?' Greg demanded impatiently. 'If we hit them now I might be lucky enough to get my cattle back.'

'If we do it right we can put an end to this trouble before it spreads further,' Ketchum opined. 'I have to go back to town now, so why don't you ride with Ringo and stake out the rustler hideout? Stay out of sight and watch them until I show up with a posse. How does that sound to you?'

'Like a dream come true,' Greg said eagerly. 'When do we start?'

'There's no time like the present; come on, what are you waiting for?' Ringo cut in.

'Ringo knows what to do so just back

his play,' Ketchum advised. 'I'll see you later. Watch out for me, Ringo.'

Greg departed eagerly with McFitt, fired up with hope, while Ketchum rode in the opposite direction to Ash Creek.

5

Mort Hallam was annoyed when he failed to find Paul Sullivan in the land agent's office. He had arranged to see Sullivan there for they had urgent business to discuss. He stood on the sidewalk and gazed around the street. His eyes narrowed when he saw Greg Bannock riding out of town in the direction of Tented B, and for a moment he was tempted to ride after Bannock and shoot him when they were clear of town, but his common sense prevailed and he quashed the impulse. Greg Bannock had proved himself to be a top hand with a gun, and Hallam wished now that he had not pushed some of his own cattle on to Tented B in order to embarrass the Bannocks. He had not known of the attempts that had been made on the lives of Pete and Greg Bannock when he made his bid to incriminate them, and the resultant gun play had put Cliff Powley out of action for at least a month.

Where in hell was Sullivan? Hallam needed to get word to Sewell and the rustlers, and Sullivan was his only contact with the cattle-thieves. It was not known in the county that Hallam did not own the big H7 cattle spread. He was a manager, running the ranch for a combine based in Dodge City, and he had been systematically robbing his bosses for two years because they were reaping the profits of his hard work while he was being paid a pittance for his efforts. Cliff Powley had come up with the idea of using rustlers to cream off some of the stock from their own brand; he had contacted the rustlers and arranged for them to work together. The set-up had worked smoothly until Chad Sewell decided to take over some of the smaller ranches and run an offshoot legitimate business. The rot had set in when Hallam became suspicious of the extent of Powley's activities in the crooked game. The ranch foreman was evidently lining his own pockets to the detriment of Hallam's own profit margin, and Hallam was determined to put a stop to the whole deal. Once the Sewell gang was gone he could start up his own operation with different men, and he would be the sole beneficiary of the outcome.

Hallam went along to the saloon and asked after Sullivan, but the land agent had not been seen. Hallam departed, and on the sidewalk he bumped into Herb Bean, the undertaker.

'Have you seen anything of the land agent?' Hallam asked. 'He ain't in his office.'

'I ain't seen him,' Bean replied, 'but I heard he had trouble earlier with Greg Bannock and took a slug in his shoulder. He'll be at the doc's I reckon. You could try there.'

'Thanks. I took Powley to Henderson earlier. Greg Bannock shot him in the shoulder too. It's getting so you can't stick your nose out on the street these days without walking into trouble.'

Hallam went along to the doctor's house. As he reached the front door it was opened and Paul Sullivan appeared. The land agent was pale and badly shocked. He had a large bloodstain on his shirt, which had been slit open and then tied together over a thick bandage around his chest and right shoulder. Doc Henderson appeared behind Sullivan, and was giving the land agent some advice on how to live with his wound. Sullivan halted in midstride when he saw Hallam.

'I've been looking for you, Sullivan,' Hallam said. 'Why did Bannock shoot you?'

'I asked him the same question,' said Henderson. 'It's a strange business, huh? And Greg shot Powley earlier, so what's going on?'

'It's none of your business,' Sullivan said wearily. He staggered as he tried to walk around Hallam, and almost lost his balance.

Hallam grasped Sullivan's arm. 'Say, you look to be in a bad way,' he observed. 'I'll see you home. I doubt you'll make it on your own.'

'I'll look in and see you tomorrow morning at your office, Sullivan,' Doc Henderson called as they departed. 'Take it easy for a week and you should be all right.'

'Why did Bannock shoot you?' Hallam repeated as they went along the sidewalk. 'Have you been getting careless?'

'No, I haven't. And I don't know what is going on. I'm still trying to puzzle it out.' Sullivan had to clench his teeth to stop them chattering. His heart was pounding uncontrollably and his head ached. He was racked with pain, and just wanted to lie down and rest. 'He dropped in on me to ask a question, so he said, and saw something in my manner that made him suspicious. But I didn't do or say anything to put his back up. He threatened me, and when I pulled a gun on him he beat me to it and shot me. It's a wonder I wasn't killed. No one told me Bannock could handle a gun the way he did.'

'You shouldn't have drawn on him,' Hallam said unsympathetically. 'I set him up with a charge of cattle rustling, not knowing that Sewell had decided to shoot him and his pa out at their place. Then Powley got hot-headed and pulled a gun, and Bannock shot him. Now I wanta know what's going on. You can't ride out to see Sewell now, so is there anyone you can trust to carry a message? I daren't go because I don't want to run the risk of being seen with a known rustler.'

'Ketchum usually runs the errands to Sewell,' Sullivan said, 'but he left town early this morning and hasn't showed up again. Do you think he's run out on us?'

Hallam shook his head. 'I don't think so. He's running this business like he was born to it, and no one suspects a thing. You must have said something out of line to Bannock to start him shooting. I'm heading back to my place now, and you better tell Ketchum to get out there fast to talk to me.'

'Not me! I'm getting out of this deal as of now,' Sullivan said as they reached the front door of his office. 'I wasn't supposed to get actively involved, and here I am wearing a bullet hole. I don't make enough from your crooked deal to cover me against that sort of thing, so I'm shutting the office and pulling out.'

'You can't leave now,' Hallam said angrily. 'I've got a lot of time and money tied up in this deal and there's a long way to go before we can stop the operation. Don't lose your nerve, Sullivan, Bannock ain't the only one who'll be shooting at you if you quit cold. Sewell has a reputation for shooting men who don't toe the line, and if he draws a bead on you it won't be your shoulder he aims at. He takes a delight in shooting men in the guts just for the hell of watching them die in agony. Whatever you do, don't let Sewell get wind of your feelings. Play him along until the right time comes, and then get out.'

'You don't have anything to worry about, with your outfit to back you,' Sullivan protested. 'But I'm on my own, and I've got everything to lose. No sir! I'm getting out as soon as I can ride.'

'Hang on and you'll be OK in a couple of days, when you get over the shock of being shot. Just lie low and sweat it out. Tell Ketchum to come and see me out at the ranch. He'll take care of the Bannocks and then we'll have a clear trail.'

Sullivan shook his head. When he spoke his voice betrayed his great fear. 'I don't care what you say, I'm not sticking around to be a target for anyone wanting to take a shot at me. But it'll take me a few days to be in a position to up stakes, and you've got until I'm ready to ride to see how

117

things work out. But I warn you, I'll be long gone at the first whiff of more trouble.'

'Don't worry about a thing.' Hallam smiled. 'I'm gonna have a couple of guns backing me after this. Bannock has had his chance. He doesn't know it yet but he's lost out. I'll be in town again tomorrow and I'll look you up then. I'll bring in Ben Tope. You'll know him by sight. He's the gunnie with a black patch over his left eye. He'll stick around town to keep his one eye on you. You'll be safe enough with him riding herd on you. And don't tell anyone that you're thinking of quitting, not even Ketchum. Just remember that, this business you're in, nobody quits and lives to talk about it.'

'Are you threatening me?' Sullivan demanded. He began trembling, and was unable to ease his nervousness.

'Hell, no, I'm warning you. I wouldn't want to see anything bad happen to you. I need you, Sullivan, but no one else does, so stay on my side.

Now I've got to ride!'

Hallam clapped Sullivan hard on his good shoulder and departed, heading for the livery barn, leaving the diminutive Sullivan staring after him with a troubled expression on his pain-racked face. When he had saddled his horse, Hallam paused to consider. He wanted the Bannocks dead, and realized that he could not wait for the rustlers to take care of the grim chore. He rode out of town and took the trail to H7, but it was in the back of his mind to visit Tented B first and put a slug through Greg Bannock.

Greg and McFitt bypassed Tented B and headed for Hallam's H7 ranch. At first, Greg was diffident, for McFitt was a stranger and Greg's experiences of the day had made him wary, but Ringo McFitt talked freely, though not entirely truthfully, about his past.

'I've done a lot of hunting rustlers,' he confided. 'Ketchum and me, we were deputies in Arizona, and helped to break up a couple of tough gangs over that way. When we split up, Ketchum came to Kansas, and when I got tired of Arizona I drifted this way to look up my old pard. I heard, when I reached Hickman, that he was here as a deputy, and it looks like I did the right thing, because you've got big trouble on the range hereabouts.'

'How'd you meet Ketchum today?' Greg demanded.

'I smelled a campfire last night when I reached that pass through the ridge where we are heading. Being a cautious kind of a man I scouted the area, and found a bunch of men camped by a stream. I only had to listen to their talk for ten minutes before I got them pegged as rustlers. I pulled out, and this morning I was crossing your range, heading for town, when I spotted Ketchum. He told me what was going on around here. We went back to check on those rustlers but most of them had ridden out except for a couple, and Ketchum recognized Chad Sewell. We were on our way to Ash Ridge to collect a posse when we came on you, and you know the rest, I reckon.'

Greg nodded, thinking that the events as McFitt told them fitted well together. He eyed Tented B as they passed it, and worried afresh about his father, but Doc Henderson had said Pete would survive. Greg steeled himself to look into the future, and vowed to end the trouble before his father could get back on his feet.

'I'm hoping to get my herd back,' Greg said as they approached the pass. 'The rustlers are stripping the range bare, and I don't think they'll run the cattle off to market until they've finished operations around here. With any luck I'll drop on to where the stock is being held.'

'I don't think you'll see your cows again,' McFitt opined, and his eyes glinted when he thought of the place where the animals were being held — deep on H7 range, courtesy of Cliff Powley. 'Those rustlers won't be holding them within fifty miles of here.'

'If they are around then I'll find them,' Cliff said resolutely. He drew his pistol and checked the weapon, aware that McFitt was watching him closely.

'The only thing you'll do with any certainty is get yourself killed,' McFitt observed. 'I can tell you that those rustlers are mighty tough men. You'd better approach them with real caution and respect.'

'I won't underestimate them,' Greg gritted through his teeth, and prayed that he would get the chance to confront the rustlers. He wanted to see them through gunsmoke, and would take his chances on coming out on top.

They neared the pass, and were about to enter the defile when McFitt stretched out a hand and grasped Greg's sleeve.

'Quick, over here,' he said urgently, reining to the left and riding into cover. 'We've got company,' he flung over his shoulder.

Greg followed instantly although he had heard nothing. He followed McFitt into a scattering of rocks until they were concealed. McFitt dismounted and stood by the head of his horse. Greg did the same, and moments later he heard a steer bawling and then hoofs thudding on rocky ground.

'Them's rustlers, I reckon,' McFitt said. 'You stay back and I'll take a closer look. I know some of the gangs by sight.'

Greg nodded. McFitt trailed his reins and sneaked off around the grey rocks, gun in his hand. Greg tried to relax, but he was intrigued. There were no steers on his range. The rustlers had taken everything when they struck. He moved forward until he could see the trail where it entered the pass. McFitt was just ahead, crouching in cover and watching intently. Minutes passed and the sounds of horses and cattle became louder. A rider passed across Greg's position, heading into the pass, and he was followed closely by a dozen steers. Greg saw the H7 brand on the animals and nodded. These were the animals

Hallam had said had been penned on Tented B.

Two more riders went by behind the cattle. They were strangers to Greg, but he would know them again, he thought grimly. McFitt came back to him, holstering his gun. He was grinning.

'I recognized one of them,' he said. 'He rides with Chad Sewell. Things must be getting pretty poor around here if all they can steal now is a dozen head.'

'I saw the H7 brand on the steers,' Greg said. 'They must be the stock Hallam saw penned up on my range. He accused me of stealing them.'

'Hallam did? Huh, that's an old trick. So what is Hallam up to? It looks like he wants you off your range.'

'That's what I thought. Hallam's foreman, Cliff Powley, drew on me in Ash Ridge, and I shot him in the shoulder.'

'You shot Powley, huh?' McFitt nodded his approval. 'You've done pretty well, Bannock. We'll follow this bunch through the pass and see what they get up to. If the rest of the gang haven't come back we could deal with these three and leave fewer for the posse to handle when Ketchum shows up.'

They waited until McFitt became restless. 'I'll ride ahead,' he said eventually, 'to check they're clear of the pass and see if the rest of the gang have shown up again. I reckon most of them are out on another raid somewhere. Keep your hand on your gun when you come up the pass. It'll be just your luck to get halfway up and have a bunch of steers following in behind.'

McFitt rode into the pass and continued. Greg waited several minutes before following, and he was tense and ready for action until he reached the crest and saw McFitt waiting there.

'They've taken the steers along the trail to Hallam's ranch headquarters,' McFitt said.

Greg could see a cloud of dust in the distance, marking the progress of the steers. He frowned.

'Are they working for Hallam now?' he asked. 'They're driving H7 stock into the ranch. Rustlers wouldn't do that.'

'It seems to be unreal.' McFitt grimaced. 'I think I'll trail them and see what comes out of it. I reckon you'll be more interested in the rest of the rustlers. Put your horse off to the left of the pass and walk in to where the gang has its camp. Circle wide and try to avoid any guards they might have out. Check on how many rustlers are at the camp, and come on back here to your horse and wait for me to get back. That way we'll have a good idea of what's going on.'

Greg agreed and McFitt departed, following the moving stock towards H7. Greg tethered his horse in cover beyond the pass and went forward on foot, watching his surroundings alertly. A heavy silence encompassed the area. There was no sign of life. Greg had seen the roof of Hallam's line shack under a stand of trees, and approached it to discover that it was deserted. He moved around it and took a circuitous route to a stand of trees many yards north of the shack. He watched for guards as he closed in, but found no one.

There was plenty of evidence that a group of men had stayed for several days at the campsite. Greg moved cautiously around the perimeter before entering the camp. He found the remains of a fire in the centre of the clearing; its embers still hot. But there were no blankets or cooking utensils around, and he checked the ground closely for tracks. He found signs that half a dozen horses had moved out to the north; he tracked them until they cleared the trees, nodding and smiling knowingly when he saw that the trail changed direction as soon as it crossed the nearest ridge. The rustlers had headed west, towards H7.

Greg returned to where he had left his horse. He was racked by impatience.

He dearly wanted to get to grips with the rustlers, knowing that he had to strike fast if he were to recover his stolen stock. Ketchum seemed to be taking his own sweet time in getting a posse together, and Greg sensed that if he handled this problem with common sense he could win the fight. He swung into his saddle and followed the small herd being pushed towards H7.

He had ridden on H7 range many times before and knew his way around. It did not take him long to get within sight of the dozen or so steers being driven to Hallam's ranch. He rode quickly into cover when he spotted Ringo McFitt riding alongside the rustler covering the drag. McFitt was chatting easily with the rustler, and dark suspicion flared in Greg's mind. What was McFitt doing with the rustlers? Greg hung back and watched intently. He noticed that McFitt kept glancing along his back trail, as if concerned that he might be seen in this company.

Greg trailed the steers all the way into Hallam's home pasture. When he came in sight of the big ranch house he circled it to avoid being seen, and saw McFitt turning into the ranch yard. Several cow punchers were at the headquarters, two standing in front of the big barn behind the house and three more at the corral, where another man was putting a half-broken horse through its paces. McFitt dismounted at the porch of the house and stepped down from his saddle.

Two men emerged from the house. Greg recognized one of them as an H7 rider. The man greeted McFitt like a long-lost friend. Greg remained in cover, wanting to check out McFitt, for he was having serious doubts about Ketchum's alleged long-time friend. When McFitt went into the house with the H7 man, Greg began to feel that he had been hoodwinked by Ketchum.

Was Mack Ketchum playing a double game? Why had he shown up at Tented B just after Pete was supposed to have been murdered? Had he been expecting trouble at Tented B? Was he involved with the rustlers? And McFitt was acting strangely — much too friendly with the rustlers. Was there any truth in what he had said about his anti-rustler work in Arizona? Greg could not begin to understand what was going on, and he was barely able to contain his impatience. But he was not about to ride into the ranch for a showdown with these men. All he could do was watch points.

He eased back into deeper cover and dismounted, then crawled forward to watch the ranch yard. He studied the three rustlers who had driven the steers into the ranch. They finished their chore and then went to the cook shack beside the bunkhouse, They trooped inside as if they were members of the H7 outfit. Greg shook his head as he considered. He did not like the direction this business was heading. He began to feel that his safest course would be to depart and pretend ignorance until he could work out what was going on.

Greg turned away and fetched his horse. He mounted and circled to head back to the pass, staying well away from the trail he had followed in. He watched his surroundings intently, not wanting to put himself at a disadvantage with these desperate men. They had tried to kill his father, and would not hesitate to put holes in him if they thought he had become aware of McFitt's apparent trickery.

When he reached the pass, Greg put his horse in cover where McFitt had told him to, and sat in the shadow of a pine tree to await the man's return. The afternoon was wearing away and his impatience grew with each passing minute. But he waited, despite every nerve in his body crying out that he was being bluffed. His thoughts wandered and he considered Ketchum's part in this business. If McFitt was crooked then surely the deputy was playing a double game. He had said that McFitt had worked with him in the past. The more Greg thought over the situation the stronger his suspicions became. He watched the trail to H7, and when he spotted McFitt riding towards him he wondered how he should handle the situation.

'Did you think I'd got lost?' McFitt demanded when he reined up in front of Greg. 'I stuck around up there as long as I could to see what was going on. Those rustlers turned the steers into the home pasture at the ranch, and they sure seemed to be on friendly terms with the H7 crew.'

'Are you sure they were rustlers?' Greg asked. 'Maybe they were some more of Hallam's crew. He's been taking on extra riders.'

'I recognized one of them as a rustler. But he might have got himself a job on the ranch to get in on the inside. Rustlers do work their way into the big outfits.'

Greg watched McFitt's face as he talked in his glib way, keenly aware that the man was lying. He was tempted to confront McFitt with his suspicions and, when McFitt fell silent, Greg eased his hand towards the butt of his pistol as he spoke.

'You're lying, McFitt. I followed you to H7 and watched from cover.'

McFitt froze and his expression hardened. He gazed at Greg with tension seeping into his big frame, and his eyes chilled. Then he heaved a sigh and laughed.

'OK,' he said. 'I guess I would be suspicious if I saw you in similar circumstances. But I went in there because I needed to see if Chad Sewell had ridden in. He's bossing the rustlers, and we need to clean up on him when the posse shows up.'

'And was he there?' Greg prompted.

'Yeah, I saw him right enough. I'd know him anywhere. I told him I was looking for Hallam, and he said the rancher was in town.'

'So what was Sewell doing at H7?'

'I didn't ask him. I got out of there

but fast. If Ketchum shows up pretty soon with a posse we can nail all the rustlers in one swoop. How does that sound to you?'

'I don't like the sound of it,' Greg told him. 'I saw the way you spoke to those rustlers, and they acted as if you and they were buddies. So what is going on and where does Ketchum fit into this crooked game?'

McFitt expelled his breath in a long sigh. He lifted his shoulders and then let them slump. His grin was fixed to his lips.

'OK!' he said. 'That settles it, I guess.'

He reached for his pistol, his hand moving in a blur. Greg was watching him intently, and set his own hand into motion, fast and smooth. He grasped his butt, cocked the big weapon as it slid clear of the holster, and levelled it in one fluid movement. He fired without seeming to aim. The noise of the shot was deafening in the heavy silence pressing in around them. McFitt was fast, but he had barely cleared leather when Greg's slug smacked into his chest. His gun flew from his hand and fell to the ground. McFitt fell sideways and slumped out of his saddle. He hit the ground with a thump and rolled lifelessly, blood dribbling from the big hole in his heart.

Greg remained frozen for several moments, shocked by the turn of events. Then he swung out of his saddle and crossed to McFitt. The big man was dead, his eyes half-open and staring sightlessly at the brassy sky. Greg drew a deep, unsteady breath and looked around, aware that it was time he moved on. In the back of his mind he knew he would need to have a reckoning with Mack Ketchum, who seemed to have a lot to answer for. He had somehow to get ahead in this crooked business, and it looked as if he would have to do it the hard way.

6

Mack Ketchum rode into Ash Ridge as the sun went down. The main street was shadowed but quiet. He put his horse in the livery barn and saw to its needs, then walked to the big saloon, the Golden Saddle, for a beer to wet his whistle before letting his thoughts turn to food. There was a gathering in the saloon and he soon picked up the thread of the conversation. He was not popular with the townsfolk mainly because of the way he acted on a Saturday night when everyone was trying to have a good time. He always had an eye open for a quick profit, and the more drunks he could cram into the little jail behind the law office the more money would be taken in fines to be shared with Judge Garland on Monday morning. He frowned when he learned fresh details of the shootings that had occurred around town during his absence.

Much of it he had already garnered from Greg Bannock, but Ketchum was not pleased as he listened. His main interest was to get rid of Chad Sewell, for the rustlers were cramping his style, and he knew he could not handle all of them together. He needed Ringo McFitt, and the plot they had arranged was the best he could do at a moment's notice. He saw several of the men present throwing glances his way, and he stemmed the wave of impatience that swept through him. He'd had a good thing going in Hickman County, but the attempts by the rustlers to get rid of the Bannocks had started a trail of events that threatened to upset the apple-cart.

A hand touched his arm and he glanced at Mort Hallam, who had approached him silently. The H7 rancher looked as if he'd been knocking back a sizeable quantity of the saloon's liquid stock. Hallam's eyes were bleary, his face blotched, and he was unsteady on his feet.

'Where the hell have you been all day?' Hallam demanded, pulling on Ketchum's sleeve. 'There's been hell to pay around here, and never a sign of you. But that's usual, huh? You're never around when the chips are down. Now you're standing here pouring it down your neck when you should be laying down the law. We've got big trouble, and if you don't do something about it pretty damned quick then we'll all be up a gum tree.'

'Keep your voice down, for Chrissakes!' Ketchum spoke in a fierce undertone. He glanced around and was relieved to see that no one was within earshot. He shrugged Hallam's hand off his arm. 'And what the hell are you pawing me for? If you wanta know what I've been doing then come along to the office and I'll tell you in private. What's biting your tail, huh?'

'It's Sullivan, among other things,' Hallam said hoarsely. 'I never liked the little weasel. I always thought he wasn't suited to the work you've given him. He's got a yaller streak down his back a mile wide. I spoke to him earlier, after Greg Bannock shot him in the shoulder, and he was talking of quitting cold. He's gonna hit the trail, Ketchum, and he talked to me of dropping in on the sheriff in Hickman to spill the beans. I think I've talked him out of his panic, but I don't trust him an inch, and there'll be big trouble blowing up if you don't put a kink in his tail.'

'I saw Bannock out on the range and he told me all about it.' Ketchum spoke tersely. 'Why don't you head back to H7? You look like you've had all you can hold. I'll do what's necessary, don't you worry, and I don't need you telling me what I should or shouldn't do. Now leave me in peace. The only thing on my mind right now is grub, and I don't want the likes of you spoiling my appetite. Get the hell out of here. I'll ride out to your place maybe tomorrow and talk to you some more.'

139

Hallam saw the killer expression in Ketchum's eyes and drew back. He had a great respect for the deputy.

'I'm not trying to tell you your job, Ketchum,' he said in a low tone, 'but you need to know what's going on around you. I've got more to lose than you, and I need to look after my interests. Keep an eye on Sullivan or this whole danged game could blow up in our faces. Bear in mind that you stand to lose a lot if that happens.'

'I'll talk to Sullivan, never fear,' Ketchum said grimly.

'Then I'll see you out at my place some time.' Hallam turned away, cuffing sweat from his brow.

Ketchum watched the H7 rancher go back to a table across the wide room. He suppressed a sigh, finished his drink and departed. After a meal in the diner he emerged and stood on the board-walk to look around the street. His mind picked over the salient points of the rustling scheme they had going, listing his likes and dislikes. He hated

Chad Sewell, but the knowledge that he and McFitt would kill off the gang boss satisfied him and he began to think of gathering a posse to ride back to the pass. But first he had a couple of minor details to handle.

He walked along the street to Doc Henderson's house and knocked on the door for admittance. Henderson opened the door, and nodded a greeting.

'I guess you want details of the men who were shot today, huh?' the doc demanded.

'I already know all I need for the record,' Ketchum replied. 'Sullivan was plugged, and so was Powley. What I want to know is where they are. I want to talk to them.'

'Sullivan went home. He ain't too badly hurt. Powley was hit harder, and he's in Mrs Gibson's guest house. He'll be there at least a week. Hallam had paid his board and told him to rest until he's able to sit a saddle again.'

'And where's Sullivan?'

'He went home. You know he lives over his office?'

'Yeah, I know. Thanks, Doc. See you around, huh?'

'I'm hoping we've seen the worst of it now,' Henderson mused. 'What's happening out on the range?'

'There's a rustler gang operating in the county but I reckon we'll bust them up before too long. I'm gonna ride out with a posse some time before dawn.'

'That's good news.' Henderson nodded and closed his door.

Ketchum went back along the street to the Gibson guest house, which was situated just beyond the general store. He found Mrs Gibson in her kitchen, cleaning up after the evening meal. Clara Gibson was a motherly type, a widow in her late fifties, almost as broad as she was tall, and she smiled at him when he caught her attention.

'How can I help you, Mr Ketchum?' she enquired.

'I need to talk to Cliff Powley,' he said.

'The poor man is resting in his room,' she replied. 'I've got to go up for his plates, so if you'll follow me I'll show you the way,'

Ketchum followed her up the stairs and into a room at the end of a short corridor. Cliff Powley was lying in bed. Blood stained the bandaging around his right shoulder. He seemed to be in considerable pain, grunting and groaning as he shifted uncomfortably. Sweat beaded his forehead, and he glared at Ketchum as if the deputy was responsible for his condition. Mrs Gibson picked up the plates and departed. Ketchum stood beside the bed, looking down unsympathetically at Powley.

'Why in hell did you draw on Greg Bannock?' Ketchum demanded. 'Ain't there enough trouble right now without you adding to it?'

'I thought I could shade him,' Powley grated. 'Hallam was pulling his gun, and I had to do something to keep him from getting killed. If we lose Hallam we lose everything. You should have been around, Ketchum. Why the hell weren't you?'

'I had things to do out of town.' Ketchum grimaced. 'Hell, I can't turn my back for two minutes without something going wrong. I'll be plenty glad when Sewell cleans out this range and pulls his stakes — I might get some peace then.'

'It's Sewell wanting to buy up ranches that's causing the trouble,' Powley snarled. 'I was playing it quietly, but Hallam had to try and get clever. He penned some H7 steers on Bannock's range to make trouble for Tented B, and it went sour on him. Nobody told us Greg Bannock was hell on wheels with a gun, and we didn't know Sewell had given orders for the Bannocks to be killed.'

'And Greg Bannock surprised everyone.' Ketchum grinned. 'But it's all in hand now. There are gonna be some changes in the set-up. We'll get back to good old-fashioned rustling, and the gang will move on when they've cleaned up.'

'I'll be pulling out soon as I can sit a saddle,' Powley said through his clenched teeth. 'I can see the game is played out around here. Hallam has got greedy. He's heading for a fall and he can't see it. I've tried telling him but he won't listen.'

'I've talked to him already. I reckon he'll toe the line now. You better stick around, Powley. We've got to see this thing through. There's still a lot at stake, and I don't intend to lose anything. I'll probably move on myself after this, so hang in there. It can only get better.'

'I'll think about it.' Powley shook his head. 'It's all right for you to talk, but I'm the one lying here, and it don't look so good from this position.'

'It would look a lot worse if I have to start gunning for you,' Ketchum rasped as he turned to the door. 'Just do like you're told, huh?'

Ketchum departed and made his way to Sullivan's office, which was in darkness. He stepped into the street and looked up at the upper windows, where lamplight was showing. Outside stairs ascended from the alley to the apartment above and Ketchum mounted them silently. He tapped at the door and waited, then tapped again, louder, when there was no reply. Moments later he heard Sullivan's voice on the other side of the door, querulous and fearful.

'Who's there?'

'It's Ketchum! Open up, I need to talk to you.'

The door was unbarred and opened a fraction. Sullivan's face appeared in the narrow opening, his taut features limned with fear as he peered out at the deputy.

'Where have you been?' Sullivan demanded irritably. 'I've been waiting all day for you to show up.'

Ketchum thrust the door wide, forcing Sullivan to step back, and crossed the threshold. 'What in hell did you do to get Greg Bannock shooting at you?' he demanded. 'You were told to lay low around here. So what happened?'

'I don't know,' Sullivan quavered. He pressed his left hand against his bandaged right shoulder and stifled a groan of pain. 'I didn't say anything. He asked me a couple of questions, and then said I looked guilty as hell about something and started to rough me up. I thought he was going to kill me. When he left I tried to shoot him in the back but he turned before I could draw a bead on him and shot me in the shoulder.'

'You're lucky he didn't kill you. He's killed four men today that I know of, and wounded Cliff Powley. You must have said something that started him off.'

'I didn't,' Sullivan snapped. 'He's gun crazy, like a lot of men around here, and when I can sit a horse again I'm getting out. I'm not getting in any deeper, and you can tell Sewell that when you see him.'

'You know the rule.' Ketchum grinned. 'Nobody quits. Try it and you'll get a bullet where you can't digest it. If I tell

Sewell you're through he'll come for you — he likes nothing better than shooting a man in the guts. You'd better think again, Sullivan. My advice to you is stay put, keep your mouth shut, and you might live to see the end of this. Turn chicken and you'll wind up on boot hill. I don't need you playing up right now. I'm heading out with a posse before sunup, and I don't wanta leave any unfinished business around here. You're not the only one in this game, so stay put. Do you get that?'

'I can't go anywhere right now, can I?' Sullivan shouted. 'When I took this job I was told I'd be protected, but I might have been killed today.' He suppressed a shudder at the memory of facing Greg Bannock, and his fears began anew. 'No,' he said determinedly. 'I'm getting out of here the minute I'm able to travel, and nothing anyone can say will change my mind.'

Ketchum sighed heavily. He stood head and shoulders over Sullivan, and was some thirty pounds heavier. He reached out a large hand, grasped the front of Sullivan's jacket, took up the slack, and shook the smaller man until his head rolled around on his shoulders. Sullivan cried out in pain as his wounded shoulder thumped against the wall at his back. He slid his left hand into his jacket pocket, gripped the .41 derringer concealed there, and jerked it into the open, intending to thrust the muzzle against Ketchum's chest and fire the weapon.

Ketchum caught the movement of Sullivan's left elbow bending and anticipated the move. He blocked the draw with his right hand, slid his fingers around Sullivan's wrist and pushed the muzzle of the derringer away from his body. Sullivan tried to resist the move but was not strong enough. His index finger, trapped against the trigger of the derringer, contracted convulsively against the curved sliver of metal. The muzzle of the pocket gun was covering his chest when the weapon exploded, and he jerked as the .41 slug smashed between two ribs and bored through his heart. He died with the thunder of the shot blaring in his ears.

Ketchum stepped back, releasing his hold on Sullivan's wrist. The little man slumped to the floor with blood spurting from his wound. Ketchum gazed in shock at the motionless body, his ears ringing from the crash of the shot. He was unable to believe what had happened. He did not need to examine Sullivan. He could see the man was dead. He shook his head in disbelief, bent and picked up the derringer, which had fallen from Sullivan's hand, and stuffed it into his back pocket. He stepped outside the apartment, closed the door gently, and descended the stairs to the street. Sullivan would keep until tomorrow.

★   ★   ★

Greg left McFitt lying where he had fallen and went to his horse. He swung into the saddle, then paused. What should he do? Indecision gripped him and he looked around. McFitt's motionless body was in full view of anyone using the pass but he decided against moving it. He would have to confront Ketchum. He needed to know what McFitt had in mind when he died. They were supposed to have confronted Sewell to kill him, but it looked like a trap had been planned for Greg himself, and he reasoned that Ketchum knew about it.

The sound of hoofs cut through Greg's musing and he swung his horse to face the direction of the sound. A gun blasted and he heard the crackle of a slug whipping by his head. He raked his spurs along the flanks of his horse and lit out fast, away from the pass, heading for cover on H7 range with a fusillade of slugs rattling fast and furiously, filling the air about him with flying death. Greg pulled his pistol and swung in the saddle. Three riders were coming from the direction of the H7 headquarters, and he wondered if this was another aspect of McFitt's perfidy. He triggered his gun, and saw the riders duck and scatter.

He faced his front, ducking as his horse passed under a tree with a low branch sticking out. The branch missed him but scraped his back, and he almost lost his seat. He swung away, heading for deeper cover, and more slugs came buzzing around him like angry bees.

It was obvious now that he had been set up by Ringo McFitt, and Greg came to the conclusion that Ketchum must have given orders to that effect. He looked around as he reached open range, and sent the horse on at its fastest pace. When he looked back he saw his pursuers following at a safe distance. He headed for timber, entered its shade, and looked around for a hiding-place. A gunshot split the brooding silence but he did not hear the ominous crackle of a closely passing slug, and wondered who was shooting at whom. He swung his horse and eased back towards the fringe of the woods, looking for his stalkers.

They were bunched and riding slowly, obviously tracking the prints of his horse. He shook his head and turned the animal, heading deeper into the timber, riding hither and thither to leave a false trail through the pine needles, pausing several times at soft patches to leave hoofprints pointing in the wrong direction before heading for higher ground in search of bare rock. He emerged from the trees and reached a hogback ridge, which he followed before cutting back into the trees and making for H7 range again, intending to descend the pass eventually and head for Ash Creek. It was high time he confronted Mack Ketchum.

He had lost his pursuers, and continued. Darkness approached, but he was familiar with the country and knew his position exactly. He needed to hit the pass during the night, when the shadows were dense, and when he reached Tented B range he could head for town. He stayed clear of the trails around Hallam's ranch and moved slowly. He was tired, and struggled to stay awake, but living dangerously pushed him to a high peak of alertness, and he was keenly aware of his surroundings as he neared the pass.

When he reached the spot where he had killed McFitt, Greg walked his horse into the cover of the H7 line shack, tethered the horse, and moved slowly in the direction of Sewell's camp. He expected it to be deserted, but caught the tang of wood smoke on the breeze and dropped into cover. He scanned the area, saw firelight flickering under the trees that concealed the rustler camp, and crawled forward until he could observe the site.

There were four horses tied to the rustler picket line. Two men were sitting by the small campfire. Greg closed in, easing forward on his belly, wondering where the rest of the rustler gang had got to. Perhaps they were out on another rustling raid. He eased forward until he was only yards from the two men, who were cooking food, the smell of which made Greg realize that he was famished. He was tempted to brace the men and take them prisoner, but smothered the impulse. It would be just his luck to start something and then have the rest of the gang riding into the camp.

Greg edged away and returned to his horse. With the gang gone and the two men in the camp being fully occupied with preparing their meal, this would be the ideal time to negotiate the pass. He led his horse out of the cover of the line shack and paused to look around. He saw nothing but silent shadows. He listened intently for unnatural noise, his ears strained for the slightest suspicious sound, but the night was still.

His eyes were accustomed to the darkness and he led his horse away from the line shack until he judged he was out of earshot of the two men in the camp, then swung into the saddle, checked his pistol, and rode to the pass.

He was on the point of entering the pass when a voice called a challenge from the surrounding shadows.

'Sit that horse and declare yourself, mister. We got you covered. We know who you are so give up.'

Greg reined in, pulled his rifle from its boot, and dived sideways out of his saddle on the side of the horse furthest away from the challenge. A gun flamed and crashed, throwing raucous echoes through the shadows. Greg landed on his left side, and as he worked the mechanism of his long gun he heard the sickening smack of a slug striking his horse. The animal squealed and went down with threshing hoofs. Greg rolled clear and got to his hands and knees. He scurried into the mouth of the pass and dived behind a rock with slugs splattering around him.

He was not touched by the questing lead, and lay motionless with his head down until the echoes began to fade into the distance. A cool breeze blew on the back of his neck — an updraught from the lower range. He pushed his rifle forward, his eyes narrowed to pierce the darkness. Starlight took the edge off the blackness of the night and he watched the approaches to the pass. He guessed that somewhere along the line the three riders who had been chasing him earlier had taken a chance on his returning to the pass, and they had caught him on the last leg of his wandering.

'Hey, you,' called the voice that had challenged him. 'You can't get away. We have a couple of guards at the bottom of the pass at night, just in case, so throw down your guns and come out of there with your hands up. We saw you kill Ringo McFitt, and you're gonna pay for that.'

Greg slid away from his cover and moved deeper into the pass. He had no intention of surrendering. He knew every inch of the pass and descended through the shadows without a problem, gripping his rifle in his right hand and moving silently. So the pass was guarded at the bottom end! He kept moving, covering a descent of about 200 yards before catching the smell of tobacco smoke on the breeze.

Greg hunkered down behind a rock on the right-hand side of the pass, which was wide enough to permit four horses to traverse it abreast. He heard the mumble of voices coming from below. The rustlers down there had been alerted by the shot fired at the top of the pass. Waiting in silence, Greg heard the ominous sounds of men descending at his back. He transferred his rifle to his left hand and drew his Colt.

'Hey, Charlie, someone's coming down the pass,' he heard a voice call from below.

'Shut your fool mouth; let 'em get here, and then challenge them,' another replied.

Silence ensued. Greg inched forward, keeping in cover where he could. He pictured the exit from the pass as he had last seen it, and knew it was screened by rocks and boulders around its mouth. He guessed the two guards would be in position on either side to lay a cross fire upon anyone descending. It looked as if he was well and truly bottled up, but he was not ready to surrender, and he edged closer to the bottom of the pass.

A rider was descending the pass at his back. Greg listened for a moment, pinpointing the sound although he could see nothing in the darkness. Then a voice called from higher up.

'Hey, Charlie, are you down there? We got Greg Bannock pinned in here between us. Watch out for him. He's a slippery cuss. He killed Ringo. We're coming down to drive him towards you. Don't shoot us.'

'Come right ahead,' replied Charlie. 'We'll pick him off.'

Greg marked the spot where Charlie's voice came from and closed in slowly, his pistol cocked. He caught another whiff of cigarette smoke, and then saw a glowing red end in the darkness only a few yards ahead. He lifted his gun and fired instantly, aiming a foot below the giveaway glow. Muzzle flame speared through the shadows and he closed his eyes to avoid being dazzled. He heard a thin cry of agony above the rolling sound of the shot, and then a gun to his left, on the other side of the pass, hammered quickly, throwing several shots at his gun flash. Greg dropped flat and scrambled forward, intent on getting out of the trap. A gun opened fire on him from behind and higher up, and he heard slugs smacking against rocks around him before whining away.

Aware that he could not stop now, Greg clenched his teeth and ran out of the pass accompanied by crackling bullets. He threw himself down into cover to the right, his lungs palpitating; his breath rattling in his throat. The second guard had to pause and reload his weapon, and when he started shooting again, Greg drew a bead on his gun flashes and fired. The guard ceased fire instantly, and Greg took the opportunity to gain more distance from the mouth of the pass. He ran into the rocks where he and McFitt had left their mounts earlier, and heard a horse stamp on hard rock. The animal whinnied, and Greg went forward silently, his Colt ready.

He came upon a tethered animal, untied it, and swung into the saddle. A rifle cut loose at him from the top of the pass, raking the area speculatively. He ducked and threaded his way through cover, burst out on to open range, and rode fast towards Tented B. Someone emptied a Winchester at him, using the sound of his horse as a rough guide, and although several slugs whined around him he was not touched. He urged the horse forward at a gallop until he was out of range.

Silence returned as he headed for Tented B under the cover of darkness. He had escaped the trap, but was aware that even more trouble was awaiting any move he made.

7

After Ringo McFitt had ridden off down the pass, Chad Sewell could not shake off a feeling of uneasiness that clung to his mind. He walked restlessly under the trees around his camp, thinking over the situation. He was aware that none of his gang liked the idea of taking over the small ranches he had earmarked, and dismissed them as having no ambition and no interest in anything but stealing a few cows and drinking the profits away in a saloon. He wondered if he was doing the right thing in getting rid of Mack Ketchum, for the man might still be useful, but he suspected that Ketchum was plotting against him and, anyway, McFitt was on his way and the decision for Ketchum's execution could not be rescinded. So with Ketchum gone the overall plan would have to be changed.

Sewell reached a decision and turned back to the camp, shouting at the gang to saddle up. It was time they made another raid. There were nine men in the camp, and Sewell ordered three of them to remain and watch for trouble. He led the other six into the pass, rode down to Tented B range, and headed north for Lazy F range, owned by Hank Farrant. He planned to lift Farrant's herd of 400 steers, drive them up through the pass and across H7 range, and hide them in a valley where others of his gang were holding more than 1,000 head of cattle, including the Tented B herd, before driving them to Abilene.

They bypassed the Tented B, and by nightfall were riding on Lazy F range. They halted to rest their horses and to await the rising moon. They ate cold food, and when starlight illuminated the range and a half-moon sailed up above the eastern horizon, they continued. When they spotted the lights of the Lazy F in the distance they skirted it at a distance, then went to work on their nefarious business.

Sewell had discovered days before that Farrant's herd had been gathered prior to branding, and they had no trouble locating the steers. The animals were reluctant to move at night, but the rustlers were greatly experienced, and when the herd was on the move it continued across the shadowed range in the direction of the pass. Sewell called to Rube Parker, his able sidekick, to give him instructions.

'Rube, you head this bunch into the valley and hold them there until I show up.'

'Where the hell are you going, boss?' Parker demanded. 'You need to be with us at least until we've got through the pass. I don't trust Hallam, as I've told you more than once. He could put the skids under us any time he thinks it would pay him to.'

'Just do like I tell you,' Sewell snarled. 'Where the hell do you get off — telling me what you think I oughta do? Are you running this gang, or am I? What the hell am I here for, huh?'

'OK, boss. I was only asking. Gimme a break, will you? We'll run the damn steers into the valley and stay there with them. Is there anything else you want us to do?'

'Don't get funny with me, Rube. I don't like funny men, and I don't like your tone. If you think you can do a better job than me then go ahead and prove it. If not, get on with what I've told you to do and I'll see you later. When you hit the valley you can get ready to make the run to Abilene. I got a nasty feeling under my breastbone that something is going wrong, and I want out of here for a spell. We'll sell off the steers and then come back and take up where we are leaving off now.'

Parker grunted an unintelligible reply and sent his horse after the slowly moving herd. Sewell gazed after him until he had faded into the gloom before turning his horse towards the Farrant ranch headquarters.

The Lazy F was one of the ranches Sewell wanted to take over. He had talked to Sullivan, the land agent, a couple of days earlier, and learned that Farrant was not interested in selling out, but losing his herd should make the rancher more amenable and, if the ranch buildings were burned down, the incentive to sell out would be all the greater. Sewell grinned as he planned. He didn't need Ketchum, and the deputy's absence would not be noticed.

Sewell reached the ranch buildings just after midnight. The house was in darkness and there was only a dim glow of lantern light emanating from the bunk house. Sewell dismounted out of earshot of the ranch, tethered his horse in a nearby stand of trees, and walked around the front yard to the rear of the house. He knew that Hank Farrant was unmarried and lived alone in the house, and that there were five cowpunchers on the payroll.

The night was still with just a faint

breeze blowing across the range. Moonlight silvered the ranch buildings with a ghostly gleam. Sewell worked his way silently round to the back of the house and then crossed to the barn. He stood in the shadows to one side of the barn and waited patiently, listening and watching until he was satisfied there was no guard. He entered the barn and struck a match. A lantern was hanging from a nail in a post; he touched the wick with the match and turned it up as high as it would go.

There was a pile of straw in an empty stall. Sewell grabbed up an armful and went out to the rear of the house, where he deposited it. Returning to the barn, he found several cans in another stall, examined them, and discovered that they were filled with kerosene. He spread the inflammable liquid over the pile of straw and tossed a match into it. The kerosene flamed immediately and the fire spread quickly. Sewell backed off, picked up a fresh can of kerosene, left the barn and went to stand in the shadows at the rear of the house. He did not have long to wait before smoke began curling out of the barn doorway and the flicker of the fire inside grew brighter. The tinder-dry woodwork crackled as the sun-warped clapboard caught and was quickly consumed. Within minutes the inferno had raced up to the loft, which was filled with straw and hay. Flames began to shoot through the roof and smoke billowed away on the breeze.

Sewell turned his attention to the house. He spilled the contents of the can he was carrying over the back wall of the kitchen and the pile of straw, then set fire to the straw. He moved back to a safe distance and watched the growing fire until the rear wall of the house was burning furiously. Satisfied, he withdrew and returned to his horse, well pleased with his efforts. He rode on for a hundred yards before looking over his shoulder, and his eyes glinted as he studied the inferno he had created. The barn roof had fallen in and leaping flames were roaring skywards. There was an ominous red glow at the back of the house which seemed to brighten and spread even as he watched. Before he turned away he saw several figures moving across the yard from the bunkhouse, and someone was yelling about the fire.

He rode back towards the pass, well pleased with his efforts. He caught up with the stolen herd but stayed behind the stragglers, out of sight of his gang. He estimated that by sunup they would be safely on H7 range. He tagged along until the lead steers started into the pass, then he cut away, heading for Tented B, determined to leave his mark on this range before he pulled out. He wanted to kill Greg Bannock, for the young rancher had shot the hell out of his bunch that day and there was a great need for a reckoning.

* * *

In Ash Creek, as the sun went down, Dora Jameson found her worries for Greg's safety increasing. She had watched him ride out of town, and did not like the idea of his being alone at Tented B. By the time the sun had gone down in a blaze of red-gold glory she had worked herself into such a fearful state that she could not settle to her evening chores. She confronted her father, filled with a sudden decision.

'Pa, I'm going to ride out to Tented B,' she said. 'I won't be able to sleep tonight, not knowing what's going on. Greg is all alone out there, and anything could happen to him.'

'Are you loco?' Jameson demanded. 'What do you think you can do on your own? You can't help Greg. This trouble has come upon him and he'll have to fight it alone. He certainly wouldn't want you hanging on to his coat tails and getting in his way. He's got enough to worry about without you adding to his problems. Anyway, it ain't fit for you to ride out at night, not with the trouble that's going on. How do you think I'd feel with you riding the trail alone? Forget that idea, Dora. I forbid you go. It's a crazy idea.'

'But, Pa — ' Dora began to protest, but Jameson cut her short.

'I wouldn't let you go even if you were a man,' he said flatly. 'It's out of the question. You can't get mixed up in that fight. Those rustlers are pretty damn mean, and the fact that you're a girl wouldn't stop them from shooting you. No, you'll have to contain your feelings and wait for Greg to get his job done.'

Dora retired to her room and dressed for riding, feeling that she had no option but to follow her instincts. She waited until her father went through to the back storeroom and then hurried into the store. She collected Jameson's pistol from under the counter and went out to the sidewalk. She was going to Tented B whether her father liked the idea or not.

The livery barn was illuminated by a

single lantern suspended from a hook in a post just inside the door, and Dora glanced around at the deep shadows invading the corners of the dusty building as she saddled her horse. She put her father's pistol in the saddle-bag, and, a few minutes later, rode out, sighing with relief as she cleared the town and followed the trail to the Bannock ranch. The night was dark, but the trail showed up like a pale ribbon in the shadows, and she was familiar with the range.

Two hours of careful riding brought Dora to the front yard of the Tented B. She reined in at the gate and studied the darkened ranch. No lights were showing, and she wondered if Greg was at home. She rode slowly across the yard, tense despite her courage, and when she halted at the porch she called loudly, her voice echoing eerily in the heavy silence.

'Greg, are you at home?'

She waited for a reply, listening to the fading echoes of her voice. The darkness and stillness seemed overpowering and she steeled herself to remain in control of her nerve. When she was certain that Greg was not going to answer she jumped down from her saddle, tethered the horse to a post, and took the pistol out of the saddle-bag. She held the gun down at her side as she crossed the porch to the house. The front door was not locked; she opened it and stood in the doorway, calling out again in an over-loud tone.

'Are you home, Greg?'

There was no reply. Dora felt her way into the big living room and edged forward. She was unable to see anything in the gloom, but she knew the layout of the house intimately and fetched up against a table beside the fireplace. She put the pistol on the table, felt for the lamp she knew would be there, and located the supply of matches beside the lamp. She felt easier when the lamp was flaring brightly. It was obvious that Greg was not at home, but she picked up the gun and the lamp and went around the house, checking for him. He was nowhere to be found. She returned to the big front room and sat down, wondering where he was at that precise moment.

Dora was determined not to leave until she had seen Greg, and settled herself to wait. She was highly nervous, and several times arose to pace the room. Two hours dragged by and no sound disturbed the heavy silence surrounding the ranch. Her eyelids grew heavy and, despite her tension, she struggled to remain awake. When she heard hoof beats in the yard she snatched up the pistol. A good shot, she was familiar with the mechanism of a hand gun, and checked the weapon before covering the front door with the .45.

The approaching rider dismounted with a thump of boots, then Dora heard his feet on the porch. The door was pushed open and Greg appeared. He had a gun in his hand, and paused to gaze at her.

'Dora,' he rasped. 'You're the last person I expected to see out here at a time like this. Are you alone?'

'I couldn't rest, Greg, worrying about you. Aren't you pleased to see me?'

'Not right now,' he said harshly. 'You should have had more sense than to ride the trail alone. There are some real bad men on the range right now.'

Dora's expression changed at his words and she heaved a sigh. Greg stared at her for several moments, and she could almost guess at what was passing through his mind. He seemed to be in the last stages of exhaustion. His face was dusty and tense, and his eyes had a touch of desperation in their depths. He shook his head and firmed his lips.

'I'm sorry,' she told him in an unsteady whisper. 'But I was so worried about you.'

He seemed to wilt then, and leaned a broad shoulder against the doorpost.

'It was good of you to think of me,' he replied. 'Say, you'd better stay here tonight and I'll ride into town with you in the morning.'

'You look all in,' she replied. 'Have you eaten today?'

'Heck, I can't remember.' He smiled ruefully. 'Would you start preparing a meal while I take care of the horses?'

'Anything you say.' Dora's tone was tinged with relief. 'I'll be in the kitchen.'

Greg nodded and went out to the porch. He led their two horses around to the corral and off-saddled, then permitted both animals to drink at the trough beside the corral before turning them into the stockade. He removed their bridles, then fetched a quantity of hay from the barn and pitched it over the rails into the corral. For some moments he stood motionless, listening to the horses eating their fodder. The night pressed in around him and he peered into the dense shadows, his ears straining to pick up unnatural sounds.

His mind was protesting against the incidents that had occurred during the seemingly endless day. He had lost count of the number of men he had killed, and anxiety for his father was throbbing in the deeper recesses of his brain. He wondered where Mack Ketchum had got to. The deputy was supposed to be returning from town with a posse. Greg stifled a sigh and forced his legs into motion. He went back to the house and entered silently. The smell of cooking food invaded his nostrils and he became aware of his hunger. He dropped the bar on the inside of the front door and went round the windows, closing the shutters.

Dora looked up at him with a smile when he entered the kitchen, but her eyes remained dark and fearful.

'It won't be long now,' she said. 'Why don't you go and sit down in the front room? I'll bring you a cup of coffee.'

He nodded and went to the windows to close the shutters overlooking the back yard. He dropped the bar on the back door, then paused by the inner door. Dora drew a deep, shuddering breath.

'Are you expecting more trouble?' she queried.

'I don't know what to expect any more,' he replied. 'At the moment I'm being careful. All day, men with guns have been trying to kill me, and I'm surprised I've made it this far in one piece.'

'Go and sit down before you fall down,' she advised, and he turned away, too tired to oppose her. Dora poured coffee into a cup and followed him through to the front room.

Greg sat down. Dora placed the coffee before him, then hurried back to the kitchen to watch her pots. Greg tried to relax but was too wound up. His head was aching; his pulses throbbed rapidly. He wondered if he would ever get back to being normal. He considered all that had occurred, and failed to reach any conclusions about his future actions. He leaned his elbows on the table and lowered his face into his hands. He was close to exhaustion. His eyes closed, and the next thing he knew, Dora was calling his name.

Dora set a large plate of hot food before him. Greg began to eat eagerly, and by the time he had cleared the plate he was feeling more positive.

'That was good, Dora,' he said, smiling at her.

'Another cup of coffee?' she asked, and he nodded eagerly.

As Greg drank the coffee he heard a sound out on the porch — a furtive foot putting weight on a sun-warped board that creaked under the pressure. He got to his feet and drew his pistol. He saw Dora's expression change and he held up a finger, warning her to remain silent. He blew out the lamp on the table and darkness swooped in around them. The heavy silence seemed to grip Dora by the throat and she sat frozen in fear. She gripped her pistol with trembling hands, realized that she was holding her breath, and gulped for more air.

Greg remained motionless by the table, listening intently. His heart had quickened its beating but he was calm and resolute. He heard the door handle turn slowly. Someone put pressure on the door, but released the handle when the door did not open. He heard the porch board creak again. Whoever was out there was up to no good, he thought remotely. He placed a hand on Dora's shoulder and she started nervously.

'Sit still right here, Dora,' he whispered, 'and I'll know where you are. Whoever is out there will try the back door next. I'm going through to the kitchen.'

She reached up and pressed her fingers on his hand resting on her shoulder. He responded, and then departed, and Dora did not hear him as he went through to the kitchen.

Greg moved unerringly through the darkness, and positioned himself to one side of the back door. He restrained his breathing and keened his ears. Long moments passed. His right hand grew sweaty on the butt of his pistol; he took the weapon in his left hand and wiped his right hand on his shirt. As he took a fresh grip on the weapon he heard the back door creak as someone tried to open it. The silence that followed the slight sound seemed more intense than before.

Greg breathed shallowly through his mouth. He heard a faint scraping sound outside on rough ground, and then footsteps moving away. He holstered his gun and grasped the bar, easing it upwards. The door made no sound as he opened it slowly. He drew his pistol. Cool air blew into his face when he leaned forward to peer outside. He saw a faint movement as a figure disappeared around the rear corner of the house to head back towards the porch. He closed the back door and edged forward to the rear corner.

He saw a man standing at the front corner of the house, motionless and ominous. Greg wondered if the man was alone, and dared not risk revealing his presence in case there were more intruders. He could take no offensive action in case the man was a member of the posse that Ketchum was due to bring out. He waited, covering the figure with his gun. The man moved at length, heading away across the yard to the corral, and Greg remained in cover, watching his progress.

When the man reached the corral he stood for some moments looking at the two horses inside. Greg remained at the corner of the house, half-covered by it, and called a challenge that echoed across the yard.

'You by the corral,' he called. 'I've got a gun on you. Who are you and what are you doing sneaking around here at this time of the night?'

The man hurled himself to the ground and bright red flame spurted from a pistol muzzle. Greg heard a slug smack into the corner of the house just above his head. He lifted his gun and sent two shots in reply, then he dropped to one knee to minimize his target area. Gun echoes blasted out in the silence and reverberated around the yard. The man sprang up and ran fast towards the nearby bunkhouse. Greg helped him on his way with two more shots, then reloaded his pistol while awaiting the man's next action.

A spate of shots hammered in reply, and Greg ducked as slugs smacked around him. The shooting ceased and Greg remained motionless. It was a stand-off, and he had no intention of leaving the cover of the house, because Dora was inside, alone and in the dark. He could not leave her, just in case. He waited, his teeth clenched and his anger rising. He had taken just about as much as he could stand from these men who were obviously his enemies.

The silence continued, and Greg's patience was beginning to waver when he picked up the sound of hoofs fading away in the distance from a spot beyond the bunkhouse. He did not relax. It could be a trick. He waited until the sound of the horse faded to nothing.

He felt vaguely disappointed as he returned to the kitchen, entered, and dropped the bar into place.

'Dora,' he called as he walked through to the front room. 'It's OK. Light the lamp, will you?'

He stood by the inner door until yellow light flared in the big room, then he entered to find Dora standing with her pistol down at her side. Her face was strained, pale, and her eyes seemed over-large and filled with concern.

'That shooting,' she gasped. 'Are you OK, Greg?'

'Sure,' he told her. 'I don't know who it was, but after we exchanged a few shots he rode off. I doubt if he'll come back again.'

'Who is out to kill you?' she demanded. 'They've stolen your herd and there's nothing else around here for them, so what do they want?'

'If they want me dead then it must

be because they want the ranch,' he replied, considering the situation. 'That land agent in town — Sullivan — I saw him this morning to ask a few questions and he turned nasty. He pulled a gun on me and I had to shoot him. He must know what's going on around here, so when we get back to town in the morning I'll see him again and see what I can force out of him. I'm through with pussyfooting around. I'm gonna get to the bottom of this trouble before it finishes me. The shooting started this morning, and I guess it won't stop until the fight is over.'

'Wouldn't it be better to get the law to check this out?' Dora demanded. 'They are paid to look into trouble.'

'I don't trust Mack Ketchum.' Greg's eyes glittered as he thought of the deputy. 'I think he's mixed up in this somehow, and I mean to get to the bottom of it. You'd better try and get some sleep, Dora, or you won't be fit for anything come the morning.'

'What are you going to do?' she demanded.

He laughed harshly. 'I certainly won't close my eyes this night,' he said. 'I'm gonna remain on guard until the sun shows. It's gonna be a long night, and there's no telling who else will come riding in looking for trouble.'

He sat down at the table and checked his pistol. Dora watched him for a moment, then settled down on a couch and pulled a blanket up to her waist. She closed her eyes but sleep would not come. She watched Greg, lonely and silent at the table. He seemed to be on the point of exhaustion, but he did not relax his vigilance; he was still sitting alertly when her eyes closed at last and she fell into an uneasy sleep.

8

Mort Hallam rode away from the Tented B with the sound of shooting ringing in his ears. He had stopped by the Bannock ranch in the hope of catching Greg Bannock napping, but had not relished the chore of shooting it out with the young rancher. He headed for the pass, concluding that he needed a professional to handle the gun chore, and decided to send Ben Tope out first thing in the morning to kill Greg. He began to consider how to get rid of Chad Sewell and the rustlers before setting up his own rustling gang. He returned to the trail leading to the pass, and was threading his way through a stand of trees when a harsh voice challenged him from the surrounding shadows.

'Hold up there. I've got a gun on you. Declare yourself.'

Hallam pulled up his horse. 'I'm Mort Hallam,' he responded. 'Who in hell are you?'

'It's Chad Sewell. What was that shooting I heard back there?'

'I was on my way home from town and decided to do the job you should have handled today. What happened to your men at Tented B? Did they lose their way?'

'Did you get Greg Bannock?' Sewell demanded.

'No. He's forted up in his house and I couldn't get near him. I'm gonna send Ben Tope after him in the morning because Bannock is too good with a gun for me. He damn near shot my head off when I was leaving. I didn't know he could handle a gun like that.'

'You should have set Tope on him first off.'

'What are you doing out here?' Hallam countered.

Sewell laughed harshly. 'I'm coming back from raiding Lazy F. We picked up about four hundred head, and they're on their way to the valley now. I thought, as I was around here, that I'd try for Bannock, but if you've stirred him up for the night then I'll let it slide. You better know that I'm pulling out tomorrow. We're gonna head for Abilene with the stolen stock, but I'll be back to clean up around here when we've got the cows off our hands.'

'Sounds like a good idea.' Hallam wondered if he could use the gang's absence to further his own plans. He touched spurs to his horse and continued, with Sewell riding at his side. Arriving at the pass, Hallam went ahead, and kept riding when he reached the top.

'I'll see you when I get back from Abilene,' Sewell called after him. 'You'll want your share of the dough, I guess.'

'You'll know where to find me,' Hallam responded, and spurred his horse into a canter. When he glanced back over his shoulder he saw Sewell riding towards the line shack and his face slipped into a scowl. He rued the day he had given permission for the rustlers to use his range as a hideout, but consoled himself with the thought that it was all coming to an end.

Mack Ketchum stood on the sidewalk in front of Sullivan's office and considered the situation. Sullivan's death had been accidental, as far as he was concerned, but he was not too worried. Sewell was on his way out and there would be no need for a land agent because the new rustler gang would not be buying up ranches in the county. On the face of it, Sullivan was well out of it, for he could have become an embarrassment. But dead men told no tales, and Ketchum shrugged his wide shoulders and looked around the darkened street. He would have to gather a posse together and hit the trail for Hallam's H7. He wondered how McFitt and Greg Bannock were doing. With any luck, they should have killed Sewell by now.

He went along to the saloon and looked around for Pete Hubbard, a carpenter who always rode with him when a posse turned out. He saw Hubbard at a table, playing poker, and tapped him on the shoulder.

'Hey, Pete, I need a posse to ride within the hour,' Ketchum said. 'Are you interested?'

Hubbard, a big, broad-shouldered man with sandy-coloured hair and small brown eyes in deep, wrinkled sockets, threw in his cards instantly and got to his feet.

'I'm your man,' he said in a hard tone. 'I've had nothing but bad luck tonight.'

'Get five men,' Ketchum said, 'and be ready to ride as soon as you can.'

'Where are we going?' Hubbard demanded.

'I'll tell you that when we're ready to leave,' Ketchum replied. 'I've been out on the range all day and I need to get some grub and a fresh horse, so you handle the details until I show up at the law office.'

'OK.' Hubbard hurried to the batwings and departed.

Ketchum stepped up to the bar, called for a beer. The bartender slid a foaming glass towards him. He drank deeply, paused to heave a sigh of relief, then emptied the glass and set it down. He left the saloon and went along to the diner, where he had a meal before leaving to take his horse to the livery barn. Bill Dodson, the liveryman, was in his office, and Ketchum picked up a fresh horse. He was well pleased with himself as he rode along the street to the law office, where six horses were tied to a rail. The posse men were waiting in the office.

'Who are we after, Mack?' Hubbard demanded.

'Rustlers,' Ketchum replied, 'We're riding out to H7. I've had a report that rustlers have been seen on Hallam's range.'

'Is Hallam mixed up with them?' asked Fred Baker, a lumber-yard worker. 'Cliff Powley was shot today, and he's Hallam's foreman. So what's going on, Mack? And where does Greg

Bannock fit into this? He brought his pa into town all shot up, together with the two men who shot Pete. Then he killed a stranger on the street. Are we going after Greg Bannock?'

'No. Bannock is on our side. He's out there now with an old friend of mine, and they are trying to get Chad Sewell, who is leading the rustlers. If they pull that off they'll have done our job for us, but from what I've heard of Sewell he'll be a hard man to put down, so let's ride, and put an end to the rustling.'

There was a chorus of assent and the posse men trooped out of the office. Ketchum was the last to leave. The posse men swung into their saddles and started away along the street, heading out of town. Ketchum took the lead and set the pace at a canter through the night, making for what he hoped would be the final showdown.

Ketchum felt mighty pleased with himself as they followed the dim trail across undulating range. Everything was working out in his favour. He was not worried about killing Chad Sewell. With Ringo already on the job, little could go wrong. It was Greg Bannock he was concerned about. Somehow or other he had to get rid of Bannock.

It was after midnight when the posse reached Tented B. Ketchum reined up on the trail leading to the pass and gazed through the shadows at the silent ranch only a short distance away. He was tempted to try his luck in case Bannock had returned, but he expected the young rancher to be with Ringo McFitt, and, after a moment's hesitation he rode on along the trail with the posse following.

They entered the pass and ascended to H7 range. Near the H7 line shack, Ketchum dismounted his men and explained where the rustlers were camped. They moved forward on foot in Indian file, Ketchum leading. Bypassing the line shack, they headed for the stand of trees where Sewell had his camp.

The camp site was silent and still, shrouded in dense shadow. Ketchum frowned. He had expected to see a campfire but there was not the faintest glow in the blackness under the trees. He sniffed for smoke, picked up nothing, and, considering, decided that Sewell had gone off on another raid. He told his men to go to ground.

'I'll go in alone on foot,' he explained in a harsh undertone. 'I don't want any noise or movement out here. Just stay quiet until I get back.'

The posse men got down and Ketchum moved away, heading for the tree line. He made no sound as he entered the trees, but froze when a quiet voice called a low challenge.

'It's Ketchum, Billy,' he replied instantly, recognizing the guard's voice. 'Is Sewell here?'

'He rode in about half an hour ago, changed horses, and headed for the valley where the stolen steers are being held,' the guard replied. 'We are pulling out before sunup. We're heading for Abilene with the stock, but we're coming back. Sewell ain't finished around here yet.'

'I need to talk to Sewell before he leaves so I'll ride out to the valley.' Ketchum's mind flitted over the situation. 'Have you seen Ringo around?'

'Not since he rode out for town. He won't be back until he's done whatever Sewell sent him out to do.'

'OK.' Ketchum turned away. 'I'll see you around, Billy. I've got to be riding.'

'Don't take any wooden nickels,' the guard responded.

Ketchum went back to the posse. 'We've a long ride ahead of us,' he told them. 'Let's get out of here.'

They went to their horses and rode out. Ketchum led them across H7 range, angling through the night to reach the valley where Sewell had gone.

*   *   *

Greg Bannock was not asleep when the posse reined up on the trail adjacent to Tented B. He heard the sound of hoofs and opened a shutter to peer out into the surrounding shadows. He could see nothing, but heard the concerted sound of several horses moving on through the night towards the pass. It had to be Ketchum and a posse, Greg thought. His impulse was to leave the house and fire a shot to attract the attention of the riders, but he was suspicious of Ketchum, and remained silent. When the sound of the riders faded he closed the shutter and went to Dora's side. The girl was curled up on a couch, sleeping peacefully, and he shook her shoulder.

'Sorry to wake you, Dora,' he said, 'but I need to ride out.'

'What's wrong?' Dora enquired, rubbing her eyes.

'Right now I'd like to be in two places at once,' he mused. 'I heard riders a few minutes ago, and I think it was Ketchum heading for the pass with a posse. I need to find out what he's up to, but I don't want to leave you here alone.'

'I'll ride with you,' Dora said without hesitation.

'I can't risk that.' Greg frowned. 'The men I'm after are mighty dangerous, and when I catch up with them the slugs will start to fly. I ain't about to drag you into the firing line. Would you be all right staying here with the place shut up tight?' He paused, aware even as he spoke that he could not leave her alone. 'No,' He shook his head. 'There's nothing for it but to take you along. But you're to trail me when we ride. I want you twenty yards behind me. If there is any trouble then you'd better duck into cover and stay down until it is all over. Is that clear?'

'Yes. I'd rather ride with you than stay here alone,' Dora told him.

'I'll go saddle the horses.' Greg turned to the door. 'Drop the bar when I leave, and don't lift it until I call you. OK?'

Dora nodded and Greg departed. He waited on the porch until he heard the bar drop on the inside of the door before he crossed the yard to the corral. When he had saddled their horses he led them back to the house and called Dora out. They mounted and rode towards the pass with Dora some yards to his rear. Mindful that the pass was guarded when he'd last descended, Greg left Dora in cover and rode through the rocks around the entrance to the rocky passage up to H7 range. He found and saw nothing, and returned to Dora.

'It's OK as far as I can see,' he told her. 'Follow me up the pass now, and be ready to duck. There might be a guard up above.'

'We're riding on to Hallam's range, aren't we?' Dora asked. 'Does he guard the pass?'

'Rustlers were guarding it earlier,' Greg replied. 'Let's push on.'

He began the ascent with Dora following, and was made uneasy by the sounds their horses made on the rocky ground. But they reached the top without incident, and Greg began to breathe easier. He rode to the shelter of the line shack and reined in. Dora halted at his side.

'I want you to stay here until I get back,' he said. 'I need to check a stand of trees not far from here. A bunch of rustlers had a camp there, and I need to find out if they are still around.'

'Be careful, Greg,' Dora warned.

Greg dismounted and left his horse with the girl. He walked slowly through the night towards the trees, moving silently, his hand on the butt of his holstered gun. He reached the tree line, and halted when a low voice called to him.

'What do you want now, Ketchum?' the guard demanded, 'I thought you'd gone.'

Greg remained motionless but his mind flashed over the situation. 'I'm looking for Ketchum,' he said quickly. 'He said he was coming by here.'

'He was here,' the guard replied. 'He wanted to see Sewell, but the boss has gone to the valley on Hallam's range to pick up the cattle. He's taking the herd to Abilene, but he'll be back.'

'Thanks. I've got to talk to Ketchum, so I'd better ride.'

'Hold on a minute,' the guard said quickly. 'Who in hell are you?'

'I'm a pard of Ketchum's. I was with Ringo McFitt earlier. Is he around?'

'I ain't seen Ringo since he rode out after Ketchum. Sewell sent him to Ash Creek. So what's your name,' mister?'

'Greg Bannock. I don't expect it means anything to you.'

'The hell it don't!' the guard rapped.

Greg heard the rasp of gun metal against greased leather and threw himself to one side, reaching for the butt of his pistol as he did so. The guard was shouting now, raising an alarm in the silent camp. His gun blasted, and muzzle flame spurted through the night only feet from Greg's face. Greg narrowed his eyes and triggered his Colt desperately. The night was filled with gun thunder as he hit the ground on his left shoulder. The guard's pistol belched fire again and Greg heard the slug thud into a tree trunk by his side.

He fired once more. The guard fell heavily and did not move again.

The echoes of the shooting faded quickly. Greg heard voices in the background. He scrambled to his feet, turned and ran back towards the line shack. His ears were singing from the crash of the raucous gun shots. He did not look back, and sighed with relief when he reached the shack. A heavy silence had closed in around him and now he could hear the faint rustling of leaves sounding in the night breeze. He was sweating when he paused in front of the shack, his heart thudding erratically.

'Greg, are you OK?' Dora demanded, appearing at his side. She was holding her father's pistol in her right hand.

'We've got to go on, Dora,' he replied. 'I need to find out what Ketchum is up to. It seems he's mixed up with the rustlers. I just spoke to one of them. He said Ketchum was here but went on to see Sewell, the rustler boss, who's apparently gone to pick up a herd of steers to trail it to Abilene. I'm guessing the herd is the stock that's been stolen from around here, and if that's the case then there's a good chance I can get my herd back.'

'But you can't fight the rustlers on your own, Greg,' Dora protested, 'and if Ketchum is involved with the thieves then you can't call on him to help you.'

'That's right,' Greg agreed. 'But Ketchum has got a posse with him, and they'll be honest men from Ash Ridge. I'm sure they'll help me when they learn the truth.'

'And Ketchum will stand by and let you tell the posse about him?' she demanded.

'I can't think of any other way to handle it,' Greg said.

'What about H7? Wouldn't Mort Hallam help you?'

'I'm not sure about him.' Greg shook his head. 'He penned some of his steers on my range and then accused me of stealing them. I had to shoot Cliff Powley because he drew on me. So it looks like they're mixed up in the rustling somehow.'

'Are you the only honest rancher on this range?' Dora asked.

'I'll answer that question after I've faced the men I know are crooked,' Greg replied.

'So what was that shooting I heard?' she demanded.

'I walked into a guard.' Greg drew a deep breath. 'Let's get moving before anyone else shows up. I want to get after my steers.'

He swung into his saddle and rode on with Dora following him. He had no idea of the location of the valley the guard had mentioned, but figured that he could pick up a trail at sunup. At least 1,000 head of cattle had been stolen over the past few weeks from local ranges, and if they had all passed along the same trail they should be easy to track. Daylight was not far off as Greg rode on with renewed hope for his future. He reckoned that all he had to do was take back his stolen stock and most of his troubles would be over.

The sky was turning grey-blue when he sighted the headquarters of H7. The horizon to the east was already tinged with red and gold, signalling the advent of the sun. Already the breeze was warming up. Greg reined up in cover from which he could study Hallam's spread. He saw figures around the corral. The H7 outfit was saddling up for their day's work. Greg wondered about Hallam. He was suspicious of the rancher's motives. But he could not allow himself to be sidetracked at this time. If his stolen stock was somewhere on H7 range he needed to find it, although he had no idea how he would wrest it from the gang of rustlers.

He glanced at Dora, who was following him stoically, noted her stricken face, and realized that she was close to exhaustion. Her eyes were dull and dark-circled. She met his gaze, smiled wanly, and he was tempted to call off the pursuit of the rustlers and take her back to town, but she gripped his arm.

'We'd better get on,' she said determinedly. 'We shan't be able to rest until we've got your herd back.'

'I hate dragging you around like this,' he said. 'But I can't spare the time to see you back to town, and I won't let you ride alone.'

'I understand, Greg.' She nodded. 'Hadn't we better be on our way before Hallam's riders leave the ranch? If we come up against any of them they might have other ideas about what we should do.'

He glanced towards the ranch, saw riders stringing out from the yard, and noticed that two men were turning in their direction.

'It looks as if we've been spotted,' he remarked. 'Let's get out of here.'

Dora nodded and followed Greg closely when he moved on. He swung to the right and took a straight line that would cut across any tracks heading across H7 range from the pass. The sun came up and shadows vanished. Greg rode with his gaze on the ground, looking for telltale tracks. Within thirty minutes he saw what he was seeking. The last herd to be stolen from the lower range beyond the pass had headed to the west across his line of ride, and he paused to check the tracks.

'Is this what you're looking for?' Dora asked.

'It sure is.' Greg nodded. 'About four hundred head came this way last night, by the look of it, and they're being pushed along fast. I'm gonna have to hit a gallop, and I doubt if you'll be able to stay close behind me. All I can tell you to do is follow my tracks until you can catch up. I'll locate the herd and then stop and wait for you. Is that OK?'

'It will have to do,' she replied. 'Be careful, Greg. The men you will come up against are not playing games, and your life is worth more than any herd of cattle.'

'There's a posse out this way

somewhere,' he responded. 'I'll call on them for help.'

'You'd have to kill Ketchum first,' she warned.

'Which is what I plan to do if he is in with the rustlers,' Greg retorted. He glanced over his shoulder and his lips compressed against his teeth when he saw two riders coming along their back trail. 'Two men are coming this way, and that changes things considerably,' he commented. 'You'll have to stick with me, Dora, but not too close.'

He turned to follow the cattle tracks, spurred his horse into movement, and looked back to check on Dora, who was following at a canter. He shook his head but continued, crossed a ridge, and went on across a deserted range under the blazing sun. He didn't like the thought of trouble sitting on his tail, but he was hopeful that at last there was an outside chance of retrieving his herd, and he would willingly risk his life in a desperate gamble to succeed.

At that moment he heard a slug thud

into the grass near by, and a moment later the sound of a rifle shot reached his ears. He glanced back over his shoulder, saw gunsmoke drifting from one of the following riders, and turned hastily to ride into the nearest cover, taking Dora with him. Two more shots hammered out behind them, and both slugs smacked the surrounding ground.

'We can't outrun them, Dora,' he observed. 'I'm gonna have to shoot it out with them. You go on ahead and keep your head down. I'll see if I can discourage them.'

Dora nodded, her expression showing the gravity of her thoughts. She did not stop to argue, and vanished over the nearest crest. Greg pulled his Winchester out of its saddle boot and looked around for a defensive position. This was where his fight-back against the rustlers really started.

9

Ketchum rode unerringly through the night, heading directly for the valley where the rustlers were holding the stolen stock. At sunup he was close to the mouth of the valley, and ordered his posse to take cover while he went forward to check. They rode into a gully, dismounted and, with a single thought, rummaged in their saddlebags for breakfast. Ketchum watched them for a moment, shook his head, then rode on to the valley. His thoughts were fast-moving as he passed through the entrance in the rising ground, wondering, as he rode, what kind of a reception he would get from Chad Sewell; he was aware that the rustler boss had ordered Ringo McFitt to kill him. And where were Ringo and Greg Bannock? Were they in this area trying to line up Sewell for the all-important bullet that would bring the reins of the rustling into their hands?

A figure appeared from behind a rock as Ketchum paused on the threshold of the valley to look around. Each knew the other, and Ketchum made no hostile move. The guard, with rifle in hand, came forward with a dubious grin.

'Howdy, Ketch?' he greeted in a friendly tone. 'What are you doing out here?'

'I've got a posse back aways,' Ketchum said flatly. 'We're hunting rustlers, Butch. Have you seen any around?'

'I wouldn't know a rustler if I saw one,' Butch Tulane replied, chuckling. 'Sewell said something about you being finished with us. Not going straight, are you?'

'There's little chance of that with men like Sewell around,' Ketchum said. He smiled but his eyes remained cold and hard. 'I hear you're heading for Abilene today.'

'Yeah, we are. The chuck wagon pulled out before daylight and the cattle are already on the move. We should cover ten or twelve miles today. But we ain't finished around here yet. Sewell is dead set on buying into the cattle raising business, so we'll be back, he says. If you wanta see him you'll have to hurry. He's at the camp, but he'll ride out in about an hour.'

'I need to see him before I go back to my posse. See you around, Butch.'

Ketchum gigged his mount forward and followed the trail into the valley. He headed for a shack close by a stream that meandered through the valley. Three horses were tethered to a picket line off to the right of the shack. In the distance, heading up the valley to the northern exit, the drag of the stolen herd was still in view. Ketchum nodded. It was a long haul to Abilene. He went on, and Chad Sewell emerged from the shack as Ketchum reined up before it.

'What the hell are you doing here?'

Sewell demanded. 'What's gone wrong?'

'I reckon something went wrong for us a long time ago,' Ketchum responded. He dismounted, turning his mount so that the animal did not come between him and Sewell, who stood with feet apart, legs braced, his right hand close to the butt of the pistol protruding from his open-topped, tied-down holster.

'Do you know Ringo is dead?' Sewell demanded.

'Are you joshing me?' Ketchum was taken aback by the news. 'I saw him yesterday. What happened?'

'I sent him to Ash Creek to handle some business, and somewhere along the line he picked up with Greg Bannock. I was at Hallam's place yesterday, and Ringo came in to tell me you were set on shooting me and taking over the gang. I sent him out again to nail you. Bannock was seen out back of Hallam's house while Ringo was in with me, and they met up again at the top of the pass. Shots were fired between them and Ringo was killed. Three of my boys chased Bannock, but he gave them the slip. When it was dark Bannock went down the pass, and there was more shooting with the guards I put out at night. We ain't seen Bannock since. So maybe you can tell me what is going on, huh?'

'This is all news to me.' Ketchum stepped away from his horse. 'I'm out here with a posse. We're hunting rustlers — I have to keep up appearances. The posse is camped outside the valley. They won't come in here. So it looks like we've come to the end of our trail, Sewell. You want it to end right now, huh?'

'It looks like you're set to double-cross me,' Sewell countered.

'You've got the wrong end of the stick.' Ketchum considered quickly. He was well aware that with Ringo dead his plan to take over the rustlers was hopeless. 'Someone else is sticking a horn into our business,' he mused aloud. 'Must have been Ringo, I guess. He always did have a tongue dipped in poison. He did tell me he was getting tired of rustling. So it's open between us. If you wanta pull your iron then get to it. I'm ready.'

'Were you figuring on shooting me in the back?' Sewell demanded.

'If I want you dead then I'll tell you so to your face, and give you an even break,' Ketchum said harshly. 'I've stuck my neck way out to go along with you, and if you're not satisfied then you know the remedy. Pull your gun.'

'You reckon Ringo was lying when he talked that one up?'

'Well, he's gone, so we can't ask him, and I don't think we can go on any longer with something like this between us. It's time to cut the string, Sewell.'

'I'm thinking that you are too keen to fight me, so I suspect something was worked out. You're due to collect a lot of dough from this herd we're trailing to Abilene, and yet you're ready to chance your arm against me — maybe lose your dough. That ain't like you. Ketchum; not like you at all.'

'Draw against me, and the winner takes all,' Ketchum grated.

'It would be better if you killed Bannock. He's a real pain in the butt. You have a posse with you, so go hunt Bannock. Pin a murder on him. He killed plenty of my men yesterday. Put him out of it and I'll give you a bonus when I get back from Abilene. How does that sound? Wouldn't that be better than fighting me and losing everything, including your life?'

'You ain't sure you can beat me or you wouldn't make the offer.' Ketchum laughed. 'But I'll go along with that.' He nodded his assent, thinking that he could always kill Sewell later.

'I'm heading out now.' Sewell did not take his hand away from his gun, but, certain that Ketchum would not shoot him in the back he turned and walked to where his horse was tethered to the picket line. When he was mounted he faced Ketchum again. 'See you when I get back from Abilene,' he said.

Ketchum acknowledged with a wave

of his left hand. Sewell swung his mount and rode off at a canter to catch up with the moving herd. Ketchum released his pent-up breath in a long sigh when Sewell was out of pistol range. He stepped up into his saddle, allowed his horse to drink from the stream, and then rode back to where he had left the posse. It looked like he was still in business, for the time being.

$\star$ $\star$ $\star$

Greg lay behind a crest, his Winchester covering the two riders approaching his position. As they drew nearer he recognized one of them — Mort Hallam. Moments later he recognized Hallam's sidekick. It was Ben Tope, the top gunman on H7, and the black patch covering Tope's left eye was as plain as a banner. Greg jacked a cartridge into his breech and peered through his sights. He waited grimly for the two men to arrive within earshot.

Hallam could see Greg's head, and

sunlight was glinting on Greg's rifle. He leaned sideways towards Tope, and said:

'Go straight for him, Ben. I'll angle off to the right and come up on him from the flank.'

'You want him dead, boss?' Tope demanded.

'That's the general idea. Why do you think we're following him?'

'There was someone with him when we first spotted him. It could get complicated if you don't bear that in mind.'

'I recognized the horse. It's Dora Jameson, the daughter of the store owner in Ash Creek. When we've killed Bannock we'll go for the girl and put her down. I can't take any more chances. From here on in we play the cards how they fall. Go get Bannock.'

Tope grinned. His right eye glinted. He reached up and settled his black patch more comfortably over his left eye-socket and then drew his Colt .45. Hallam swung his horse and went to the left. Greg realized what they were doing and called out immediately.

'Hold it right there, Hallam. If you've come to fight then you'll have to do it out in the open. I reckon you're in with the rustlers.'

Tope fired three swift shots at the crest where Greg was waiting. Greg ducked as the shots hammered, and dust spurted up around his position. When he lifted his head again he saw that Hallam had vanished. Tope was coming up the slope at a gallop, waving his pistol as he charged. Greg glanced through his sights, drew a bead on the tall gunman, and followed through with his aim as he fired. Gun smoke blew into his face and momentarily obscured his sight. When it drifted away he saw Tope still coming forward, but the horse had slowed its pace because the gunman was no longer controlling it, and Tope was slumped over his saddle horn, swaying drunkenly. Tope's hand and pistol were down at his side. There was blood on the front of his shirt. The next instant the gunman pitched sideways out of leather, and sprawled, inert, in the long grass.

Greg slid back from his position and ran to his left. He stopped when he saw Hallam ascending a gully in the slope. The rancher was urging his horse forward. Greg waited, and when Hallam emerged from the gully some thirty yards away, Greg covered him with his rifle. Hallam came towards him, spurring his horse, and began to yell like a Confederate rebel. The rancher lifted his pistol and fired twice at Greg, but his jolting movements affected his aim and his slugs whined over Greg's head. Greg lifted the Winchester to his shoulder and fired a shot.

The bullet struck Hallam in the body just above his belt buckle. Hallam dropped his pistol and went over backwards, his left leg pulling out of his stirrup, his right leg catching and holding as he came off the horse. His weight dragged his right leg clear; he hit the ground hard and lay still. Greg stood motionless, listening to the fading echoes of the shooting. He could see a bloodstain spreading across Hallam's shirt and knew the rancher was hard hit. He walked over to where Hallam lay and kicked away the discarded pistol. Hallam seemed to be unconscious, although his eyelids were flickering.

Greg went back to his previous position and looked down the slope at the gunman. Tope was sprawled on the ground on his left side, supported on one elbow. He was holding his pistol ready to continue the fight; he lifted the weapon when he spotted Greg.

'Throw down the gun, Tope,' Greg called, transferring his rifle to his left hand and drawing his pistol.

Tope shouted unintelligibly and raised his gun. Greg clenched his teeth and fired. Tope flopped backwards and flung his arms wide, his gun falling away. Greg exhaled in a long sigh and started down the slope to where the gunman was lying. Tope was dead. Greg viewed the lifeless body unemotionally. Then he turned abruptly and went back to where

Hallam was stretched out.

The rancher was barely conscious. Blood covered his shirt in a wide stain which increased gradually in extent with each passing moment. Hallam's breathing was laboured, his face unnaturally pale. His eyes held a glazed expression, as if he was already peering across the Great Divide. Greg's shadow fell across him and he blinked.

'Is that you, Bannock?' Hallam demanded hoarsely, and blood dribbled from his taut mouth.

'Yeah.' Greg dropped to one knee beside the stricken rancher. 'Why in hell did you start shooting? I had no quarrel with you.'

'You've done for me,' Hallam muttered. 'I know it. I've played the wrong game, and now the aces are coming up against me.'

'We're a long way from town,' Greg observed. 'You're hit hard, and the best I can do is ride to your place and get a wagon. But I don't reckon you'll make it to town.'

'Leave me lie!' Hallam shook his head; stifled a groan. A dribble of blood appeared from between his lips. He reached up and grasped Greg's hand, jerking it as if to stress what he was saying. 'I'm on my way out, I guess. I made a mistake and got in too deep with the wrong kind of people. I was doing OK until Sewell and his gang showed up. He was big time, planned to take over the whole danged county, and I got caught up in it. I couldn't break free. Now I'm down in the dust and it's too late to be sorry. Your herd is on its way to Abilene, Bannock. All the rustled stock was being held in Antelope Valley and they drove 'em out this morning. But that ain't the least of your worries. Mack Ketchum is in with the rustlers. He rode with Sewell's bunch some years ago, before he became a deputy sheriff. Watch out for him. He's got you lined up for a slug. He rode past my place ahead of you, making for the valley, and he's got a posse with him.'

223

Greg heard the sound of an approaching horse and stood up, lifting his hand to bring his gun into action. He saw Dora coming towards him. Her face was set in a mask of anxiety. He waved reassuringly to her, and when he looked down at Hallam again he saw that the rancher was dead.

'Greg, are you OK?' Dora called as she arrived. She slid out of her saddle and turned to gaze at Hallam's motionless figure. 'You've killed Mr Hallam!' she gasped, her features paling.

'The chips were down,' Greg replied. 'It was him or me, and I didn't start the shooting.'

'Why?' Dora demanded. 'How was H7 caught up in this trouble?'

'Hallam was in with the rustlers.' Greg shook his head as he considered. He thought over the rancher's last words. 'I've got to ride to Antelope Valley, Dora. The rustlers were holding all the rustled cattle there, but they've started them on the trail to Abilene, and Ketchum went along there with a posse. The trouble is, Ketchum's one of the rustlers.'

'You can't go after them alone,' Dora protested in a frightened tone. 'There will be a dozen rustlers at least, and you don't know whose side the posse will be on.'

'I'd go through hell itself to get my steers back,' Greg replied. 'But we're not going to risk your life any longer. I think it will be safe for you to head back to town.'

'No, Greg.' She shook her head. 'I'm not going anywhere alone. I'll tag along with you.'

She swung her horse round until its head was pointed towards the distant valley. Greg gazed at her for a moment, then heaved a sigh and fetched his horse. He swung into the saddle, set off at a fast clip, and Dora stayed by his side. The cattle tracks he had followed past H7 stretched out straight and plain — all pointing towards Antelope Valley.

As he rode Greg was filled with

optimism. He had a chance of retrieving his herd, and the odds against him did not enter into his thoughts. He would fight as and when he could, for no one was going to get away with his stock without a fight. He considered Mack Ketchum. He had been right about the crooked deputy all along. But what was Ketchum doing with a posse on the heels of the stolen herd? Was he going to fight the rustlers? Or did he plan to take over the herd for himself?

'You'd better drop back to a safe distance, Dora,' Greg said when they neared the valley. 'Hallam said the herd pulled out this morning, but maybe Sewell left a couple of guards behind to cover his back trail.'

Dora dropped back obediently and Greg continued, filled with determination. He rode through the entrance to the valley, checking for guards, and reined up at the sight of the wide, curving tract of land that opened up before him. He saw no cattle, but plenty of tracks. Dora came to his side.

'The herd's gone,' she observed.

'But they won't be far ahead,' Greg mused, 'and they can only make about twelve miles a day at best. What I need now is a posse to back me.'

'Ned Brewster's place is about fifteen miles to the east when we get clear of the valley,' Dora observed. 'Mr Brewster was always telling Dad what should be done about the rustlers. He was all for gathering men from the neighbouring ranches and having a showdown with the thieves. When we get through the valley, I could cut off and see if I can get him to turn out with his crew.'

Greg shook his head slowly. 'We have to hurry now,' he responded. 'We'll ride together for Brewster. I haven't got any supplies with me, and we'll be out here at least a week if we manage to grab the herd off the rustlers. I never expected to have the chance of getting my stock back, so I didn't prepare for a long trip.'

Dora urged her horse forward and entered the valley. Greg spotted the shack beside the stream and angled towards it. Dora dropped back again as they drew within gunshot range. Greg saw no horses around, and held his pistol ready as he closed in. He dismounted in front of the shack and entered the little building, finding it empty. He scouted round the area, and found nothing. The rustlers had evidently pulled out in a hurry, and there was no sign of the posse.

'Water the horses, Dora,' Greg suggested. 'I wanta look around on foot. I might be able to read something from the tracks around here.'

Dora led the horses to the stream. Greg studied the ground. There was a profusion of horse tracks, but he could make nothing of them. Some were very fresh, and all were headed up the valley. Greg was gazing into the distance when Dora returned to his side.

'What are we going to do, Greg?' she asked.

He stirred, dragging his mind from his thoughts. 'I reckon I need to get a look at the herd to see what sort of opposition I'll be up against,' he mused. 'And I'd give a lot to know where Ketchum and the posse are right now and what Ketchum is up to. Let's follow the tracks until we clear the top end of the valley.'

They rode on, and two hours later passed out of the valley on to broken rangeland. The broad ribbon of tracks left by the herd was like a signpost pointing to distant Abilene. Far ahead, Greg spotted a cloud of dust that marked the progress of the herd. He got down from his horse and checked for tracks, finding hoofprints superimposed on cattle tracks. He pushed back his Stetson and wiped his clammy forehead.

'Apart from the rustlers, it looks like six horses followed the herd out of the valley,' Greg mused. 'I guess that'll be Ketchum and the posse. I'll tell you what we'll do. You head for Brewster's place, tell him what's going on here, and bring him and his outfit running. I'll trail the herd from a distance and watch for you to turn up with help. Then we'll be able to make plans. Can you handle that, Dora?'

'Sure.' She nodded confidently. 'I reckon I won't get back to you this side of sundown. You'll have to keep an eye open for us, and we'll be watching out for you.'

'Good girl!' Greg smiled as Dora turned her horse and rode off to the east. She turned once to wave farewell and he responded. When she vanished over a distant crest his smile faded and he clenched his teeth. He set spurs to his horse, his face frozen in harsh lines, and rode resolutely, intent on getting his herd back or dying in the attempt . . .

* * *

Ketchum returned to his posse when he left Sewell, his thoughts profound as he rode. The posse was now an embarrassment to him. He could do nothing to further his plans while honest men from the town were with him. He found the posse waiting impatiently. He dismounted by the campfire, and squatted over a coffee pot boiling on the fire.

'What gives, Ketchum?' demanded Pete Hubbard impatiently. 'Did you see the rustlers?'

'How many are there?' asked Fred Baker.

Ketchum ignored their questions while he drank coffee. When he had finished, he flung away the dregs and tossed the mug to Hubbard.

'There are a dozen rustlers pushing about a thousand head of cattle towards Abilene,' he told them.

'So when do we hit them?' demanded Hubbard.

'We'll head to the top end of the valley and check the direction of the herd before I make any plans.' Ketchum turned to his horse. 'Let's make tracks.'

They rode into the valley and traversed it. Ketchum's mind was working fast. When they reined up clear of the valley he pointed to the tracks left by the herd.

'The rustlers are heading for Abilene,' Ketchum remarked. 'Let's get on and see what opposition we've got.'

They galloped across rough ground, following tracks, and eventually spotted the drag of the herd raising dust in the distance.

'I don't want to get any closer in case we tip our hand to the rustlers,' Ketchum said.

'Aren't we gonna hit them?' Hubbard demanded.

'I've thought about that and I don't think it's a good idea. The rustlers are on their way to Abilene, and we'll know exactly where they'll be until they get to market, so we can hit them any time between now and then. What I want you men to do is ride back to Tented B and see if Greg Bannock is there. He's got to be arrested for murder.'

'Any killing Greg has done would have been in self-defence,' said Fred Baker.

'You didn't mention this before,'

observed Hubbard. 'Who's been murdered, and why do you think Greg did it?'

'I have to play the cards close to my vest,' Ketchum replied. 'Don't give me a hard time. If I say Bannock murdered someone then he did, and you'd better pick him up like I tell you. Now move out.'

'What are you gonna do?' Baker asked.

'I'm gonna ride over to Ned Brewster's place and get him and his outfit in on this deal. We'll hit the rustlers just before sunup and catch them cold.'

'So we've had this long ride for nothing,' grated Hubbard. 'Do you reckon we've got nothing better to do than ride around the range looking at the scenery? We could have stayed at Bannock's place last night and saved ourselves and the horses.'

'Quit your bellyaching and do like I tell you,' Ketchum said through his teeth. 'Grab Bannock, take him back to town, and stick him in a cell. Now beat it. I'll see you when I get back.'

Hubbard glanced at his fellow posse men and jerked his head in the direction from whence they had come. They turned their mounts and rode back towards the valley. Ketchum sat his horse and watched them out of sight. When they had vanished behind a rise he continued to follow the stolen cattle, trying to work out his next move.

The posse men continued in silence. Hubbard was not happy and, as soon as they were out of sight of Ketchum, he reined in suddenly, causing the other four riders to pull in their horses.

'I ain't happy about this, not by a long rope,' Hubbard said angrily. 'I ain't gonna look for Greg Bannock. I don't know what Ketchum is talking about. He never mentioned murder until just now. And Greg Bannock ain't the type to murder anyone. I saw him shoot that gunnie in town yesterday. That wasn't murder. And the two dead men he brought into town when he toted Pete in were killed in self-defence. Then he shot Cliff Powley in the shoulder when Powley drew on him. So tell me who he's supposed to have murdered. I don't like it, and I think Ketchum is playing some deep game of his own. He seems to know a lot about the rustlers and what they're doing. And why didn't we attack that crooked bunch soon as we saw them? That's what we're out here for, ain't it?'

'I'm thinking along the same lines,' said Baker. 'And I don't mind telling you that I've had enough of this. I ain't ever gonna ride with the posse again, not while Ketchum is running it. And I ain't riding back to town through the pass. I know a short cut that'll knock ten miles off the trip to town. We don't need to go through the valley. Anyone wanta join me? I'm heading east to pick up a game trail that'll get us down the ridge, and we'll be in town by mid-afternoon.'

The others agreed and Baker took the lead, heading east.

Greg followed the herd, being careful to stay back out of sight, and watched tracks closely. When he spotted five sets of steel-shod hoofprints pull aside from the general mash of tracks he reined in, dismounted, and examined them closely. He frowned when he noted that they had turned away from following the herd. He remounted, and tracked their new direction for a couple of miles, initially thinking that they were heading back to the valley. But when they cut away east he stood gazing over the deserted rangeland, trying to decide where they might be heading.

He gave up the puzzle and returned to the spot where he had seen them break away from the herd. He had been following the prints of six horses that had been tracking the herd, and now five of them had turned back. He looked over the ground again and noted that one rider had gone on; he followed the tracks for perhaps another mile before seeing them veer off to the right. He studied the hoofprints but they told him nothing, except that the rider could be heading towards Ned Brewster's ranch.

If the posse had turned back to town then apparently Ketchum had gone on alone, and it looked like he was heading for Brewster's place. Greg frowned as he thought of Dora and wondered what might happen if Ketchum met up with her. Would she be safe? Would Ketchum put two and two together, decide that she was in league with Greg, and take steps to remove her?

Greg realized that he could not take any chances in this situation. Dora was helping him out and he had to protect her. The herd could wait. He swung away from the cattle tracks and rode fast along the single set of hoofprints he reckoned had been left by Mack Ketchum. If it was Ketchum heading for Brewster's place the showdown between them would come sooner than expected.

10

Dora rode eagerly towards the Brewster ranch, thankful to be doing something that would help Greg. She was relieved that the stolen herd was in a position to be reclaimed from the rustlers, and was certain that Ned Brewster would turn out with his crew to see that right prevailed against the bad men. She hoped that Greg would not become impatient and attack the rustlers before he had help to overcome them, but, knowing him as she did, she was afraid that he would succumb to temptation and throw away his advantage with a rash decision.

She stifled a yawn, tired by the near-sleepless night she had experienced, and the heat of the sun sapped her alertness as she continued. She was still some miles from Brewster's ranch when she cantered over a crest and had to pull her mount up sharply, for a horse was down on the reverse slope with a man lying beside it. She saw at a glance that the horse had broken a foreleg. The man had evidently been thrown when the horse fell, and was stirring as Dora dismounted quickly, trailed her reins, and hurried to his side.

'Are you OK?' Dora enquired anxiously. She looked into his face, and was horrified when she recognized Mack Ketchum. 'What are you doing here?' she demanded.

Ketchum looked up at her, his eyes vacant, but the sound of her voice brought him back fully to his senses, and his expression changed as full alertness returned to him.

'Dora Jameson!' he said. 'Where did you come from?'

Dora got to her feet, but he reached out quickly and grasped her wrist as she attempted to return to her horse.

'Hold on,' he rasped. 'I asked you a question. I'm looking for Greg Bannock, and I guess he ain't far away from you, so where is he?'

'Let me go.' Dora struggled in his grip but could not break it despite her desperation. Ketchum was in league with the rustlers, a bad enemy, and she could not afford to fall into his hands to be used against Greg.

Ketchum heaved himself to his feet, still gripping Dora's arm. He staggered as his senses reeled — he had struck his head in falling and had lost consciousness — but now he was fully alert. He looked around for Greg Bannock.

'Where's Bannock?' he demanded. 'Where have you come from? What are you doing around here? When did you leave town?'

'So many questions,' Dora countered. 'I might ask you the same. What are you doing here, looking for Greg, when there's a stolen herd on the way to Abilene a few miles back?'

'How'd you know about the steers? Who told you they're going to Abilene?'

'Mort Hallam told Greg before he died.'

'Hallam is dead?' Shock filtered into Ketchum's expression. He shook her roughly. 'You'll tell me what's going on if you know what's good for you. Where is Bannock?'

'Find him yourself.'

'What are you doing, riding out this way?' Ketchum's tone hardened. 'There's only Brewster's spread out here. So you're riding there for help, huh? That means Bannock is trailing the herd.' He saw Dora's expression change and read it correctly. 'So that's where he is, huh? And he's sent you to get Brewster to help him fight the rustlers.'

'Which is what you're supposed to be doing,' Dora rapped. 'But you're working with the rustlers. You've been helping them ever since they hit this county.'

'Who have you been talking to?' Ketchum shook Dora. 'Tell me what's going on.'

Dora did not reply. Ketchum dragged her to the side of his horse, saw the animal's broken leg, and drew his

241

pistol. He fired a shot into the animal's head. Dora flinched at the shot. Ketchum loosed his hold on her.

'I'm gonna have to take your horse,' he said. 'You can walk to Brewster's. It'll take you a couple of hours at least, and by the time that bunch turn out looking for trouble I'll be long gone, but not before I catch up with Bannock. I'll put him out of the game if it's the last thing I do. He's spoiled the whole danged business by sticking his nose in where it didn't concern him.'

Dora made a sudden dash for her horse, which was cropping the grass a few yards away, but, quick as she was, Ketchum was faster. He reached her as she jumped up for her saddle, grasped her around the waist, and dragged her away from the animal. He dropped her heavily to the ground and she lay glaring up at him, aware that her father's pistol, stuck in her waistband, was digging painfully into her left hip.

'You better start walking if you wanta get to Brewster's before sundown,'

Ketchum snarled. He gathered in her reins and stepped up into her saddle. 'See you around,' he added. He turned the horse and started back towards the distant herd.

Dora sprang to her feet, fears for Greg piling up in her mind, for she knew that Ketchum would not give Greg an even break. She looked at Ketchum's broad back as he urged her horse away, and reached for her father's pistol, pulling it from her waistband. The gun was heavy in her slim hand but she was a good shot. She lifted the weapon, aimed at Ketchum's left shoulder, and squeezed the trigger. The gun blasted and recoiled in her hand, the noise of the shot hammering away across the range. Ketchum jerked in the saddle, threw his arms wide, then pitched over sideways and fell to the ground. Dora saw a splotch of blood appear on his left shoulder blade.

For a timeless period she stood frozen in horror, breathing shallowly through her open mouth. Her horse had jumped at the sound of the shot, but after cavorting a few strides it halted and began to crop the grass underfoot. She approached Ketchum, who was inert on the ground, his face upturned to the brassy sky. He was unconscious, his features pale with shock. She could hear the echoes of the shot fading into the distance; grumbling sullenly. She drew a deep breath, restrained it for a moment, then exhaled in a long, bitter sigh. She felt sick. Her senses whirled with the dreadfulness of what she had done.

She dragged herself from the paralysis of shock that gripped her, went to her horse, and paused when she saw spots of Ketchum's blood on the cantle of the saddle. She thrust her gun into her waistband and bent to grasp a handful of grass to wipe the leather clean. As she swung into the saddle and turned towards Brewster's ranch, she caught a movement out of a corner of her eye and looked at Ketchum — saw he was sitting up and looking at her.

His pistol was clutched in his right hand and pointing at her.

'Where do you think you're going?' he snarled. 'Get rid of that gun and then get off the damn horse. I oughta kill you for shooting me. Get down before I'm tempted to put your light out.'

Dora discarded her gun and stepped down from the saddle. Ketchum lurched to his feet. He holstered his pistol and made for Dora's horse. As he passed her he swung his right hand, delivering a back-handed blow to her face that knocked her to the ground. He kept moving and hauled himself back into her saddle, stifling a groan of pain as the movement tugged at his shoulder. Dora looked at her gun, lying two feet away in the grass. Ketchum seemed to have overlooked it. She watched him. He spurred her horse and took off fast, heading back towards the herd.

Dora threw herself at her gun and clawed it up, seeming all fingers and thumbs as she cocked it and raised it into the aim. Ketchum didn't look back. He was unsteady in the saddle. Blood was spreading through the thin fabric of his shirt. Dora tried to steady her breathing. The muzzle of the gun wavered, and she feared that Ketchum would get away. Then she steeled herself for a desperate effort, restrained her breathing, and drew a bead on the centre of Ketchum's broad back. He was almost on the crest when she fired, and she flinched at the raucous crash of the shot. Ketchum fell forward over the neck of the horse and the animal halted precipitately. Ketchum pitched sideways and fell to the ground. His right foot came out of the stirrup but his left was caught, and he lay with the foot hooked above ground.

The horse did not move. It turned its head and looked at Dora as she ran to it.

Ketchum was dead, his eyes staring sightlessly at the glaring sun. Dora freed his foot and wearily mounted her horse. As she turned to ride on to

Brewster's she heard a shout from behind, and, when she looked in that direction, she saw Greg riding towards her.

Greg came rapidly to her side. He glanced down at the motionless Ketchum, shook his head, and turned his attention to Dora.

'I heard the shots,' he said. 'What happened?'

He listened in silence to what Dora said, his eyes narrowed as they watched her pale face. When she broke off and gulped he reached out and put a reassuring hand around her slim shoulders.

'Don't let this get to you,' he said softly. 'Ketchum was the lowest kind of man — working for the law and running with rustlers. You killed a snake, Dora, and if you hadn't got him then he might have nailed me. Come on, let's head for Brewster's place. It's time we threw a loop around those rustlers.'

They rode on together, and in no

time were approaching the Brewster ranch, a large spread with two barns and a sprawling house, all in good repair. A man armed with a rifle was standing in the doorway of one of the barns, gazing out across the wide yard, and he shifted his rifle from his shoulder into a readiness position as they neared the gate. Ned Brewster, a tall, thin man in his forties, appeared on the porch from inside the house at the sound of their horses. He stood with his feet apart, legs braced, and his right hand rested on the butt of the pistol nestling in the open-topped holster tied down on his right thigh.

'There's Brewster now,' Greg remarked. They slowed their mounts and trotted across the yard to rein up in front of the porch.

'How do, Bannock?' Brewster's face was grim; his dark eyes steady as he raised his hat to Dora. 'Miss Jameson, it's nice to see you. To what do I owe this pleasure?'

'There's been hell to pay my side of

the pass,' Greg said, 'and the rustlers are making off with a thousand head, heading for Abilene.'

'They tried to get in here three nights ago,' Brewster said. 'We ran 'em out, but they killed Pete Nolan.'

'I've been fighting them.' Greg pushed back his hat and cuffed sweat from his glistening forehead. 'Mort Hallam is dead. He was working in with the rustlers.'

'The hell you say!' Brewster straightened his shoulders and half-turned to motion to the guard, who was coming across from the barn. 'Hey, Tom, get the crew ready to ride. We're going after some rustlers.'

The guard turned and ran back to the barn. Brewster returned his attention to Greg.

'How many rustlers did you see?' he demanded.

'About a dozen or so.' Greg explained about Mack Ketchum and the rancher cursed.

'I never did cotton to that skunk,'

249

Brewster said vehemently. 'I always thought there was something about him that didn't tally right.' He looked at Dora and grinned. 'So you bumped off a turncoat, huh? That's the best news I've heard in a week. Why don't you step into the house? It'll be half an hour before the boys will get themselves together. Do you need food, or anything?'

'A bite of breakfast would be good,' Greg said, and went on to explain the position of the herd. They entered the ranch house. 'We've got plenty of time to pick a good spot to hit them,' he mused.

Brewster's wife was in the kitchen; a tall, plump woman with a motherly face. She greeted Dora warmly and bustled around preparing breakfast for her unexpected guests.

Brewster listened intently to what Greg had to say, then nodded. 'From what you say I expect the rustlers will hold the herd at Packrat Creek tonight,' he surmised, 'and I reckon that will be the best place to hit them. We can stampede the herd back towards the valley and pick it up later, after we've settled with the rustlers. What do you say to that? If you've got a better idea then trot it out and we'll chew on it.'

'I was thinking along that line myself,' Greg replied. 'With the herd on the run, the rustlers will hightail it. The herd will be too tired to run far, and once we've dealt with the rustlers we can hold the herd until morning and then turn it back to the valley.'

'That's the stuff!' Brewster nodded. 'We go for the rustlers and finish them off. The herd won't be going anywhere. Now you'd better eat. We'll hit the trail soon as everyone is ready. I'll go chase up my crew. I reckon you'll need a fresh horse, huh?'

Greg nodded and Brewster left the house. Greg sat down at the kitchen table beside Dora. He placed a hand over hers and squeezed it reassuringly.

'You'll stay here with Mrs Brewster until we get back,' he said.

Dora started to rise, protesting, but Greg pulled her down and gripped her hands.

'No dice!' he said firmly. 'You are staying right here.' He looked up as Mrs Brewster came to the table with plates filled with hot food. 'Could you do with some company today, Mrs Brewster?' he asked.

'It would be lovely to have Dora here,' the woman replied. 'It will be a long day waiting for the crew to come back. There will be a lot of lead flying around when you hit the rustlers, and half of it will be thrown at our crew.'

Dora subsided with resignation showing on her face. Greg patted her arm. He began to eat hungrily, and after he had cleared his plate he arose from the table and departed.

'See you when we get back,' he said, pausing at the door.

'Good luck,' Dora responded. He sighed with relief and went out, his mind slipping into the problem of fighting the rustlers.

Brewster had a dozen cowboys assembled in front of the corral — every man heavily armed. Horses were saddled in readiness for a long ride. Water canteens had been filled and saddle-bags contained supplies for a several days. Brewster was giving instructions to the cook about taking care of headquarters while the crew was away. A fresh horse was waiting for Greg. The men mounted eagerly, and Brewster led them out, setting a canter that ate up the miles. Greg was content to side the rancher, and they kept up a steady pace.

This was home range to the cowboys, and they knew time was on their side. Brewster angled north through undulating rangeland. Two hours later they ascended an incline and reined in on the crest from which they could see to the north for miles. A great cloud of dust marked the position of the stolen herd. Brewster immediately rode back beyond the crest, urging his men to do likewise.

'Well, there they are,' the rancher said with a note of satisfaction in his voice. He reined forward until just his head protruded above the crest, then reached into a saddle-bag and produced a pair of long-range glasses. He studied the distant scene before handing the glasses to Greg. 'There's a dozen of them, trailing along like a regular outfit. They've got a nerve, huh?'

Greg adjusted the glasses to his eyes and studied the herd, which was moving four or five abreast. A chuck wagon was a mile ahead of the herd. A single rider was leading the way some yards ahead of the first steers, and six riders were covering the flank and swing positions, three on either side of the moving mass of beef on the hoof. Three drag riders were bringing up the rear, smothered in dust as they darted hither and thither, chasing up steers that tried to break away from the herd and urging on stragglers.

'If we rode ahead and attacked from

the front we'd catch 'em cold,' said Brewster.

'Why don't you do that while I ride with a couple of your men and hit them from behind?' Greg suggested. 'We'll stay out of sight until you start shooting and then take the drag riders from the rear. That way, nobody will get away, and we don't have to wait for them to camp at Packrat Creek.'

'Sure!' Brewster nodded. 'I like that. Chuck, you and Joe ride with Bannock, and do whatever he says. The rest of you come with me. When we hit the rustlers we'll split into two groups and take both sides together. I don't want any rustlers to get away. OK?'

There was an eager chorus of assent. Brewster grinned at Greg and swung his horse. He rode off with his crew, leaving two cowboys behind with Greg.

'We'd better ride that way,' said Chuck Porter, pointing off to the left. 'We can keep out of sight of the rustlers until we've cut them off.'

'Lead the way,' Greg replied. They

headed to the left for a mile before coming upon a gully that led down to the bottom of the ridge. When they emerged from the gully they were just behind the herd, and moved forward cautiously, staying out of touch.

Greg could feel tension swelling behind his breast bone. He touched the handle of his holstered Colt, discovered his hand felt clammy, and wiped it on his thigh. Excitement throbbed through his mind like water in a flash flood, but he eased the pressure by thinking of his father and the men who had tried to kill him. Impatience tugged at him. His cattle were in that bunch being driven to market, and they represented everything he and his father had worked for over the years. Without the cattle they were facing ruin.

They moved in closer, waiting for the sound of shooting up ahead to set them into action. They matched the numbers of the rustlers, and had surprise on their side. They began to eat the dust rising from the hoofs of the herd, and

Greg slipped his neckerchief up over his nose and mouth. His eyes began to sting. He wondered how he would perform in a cold-blooded fight. The drag riders behind the herd were in plain sight now, moving back and forth across the rear of the herd, using their ropes to chivvy the steers forward at their best pace.

Presently shots hammered through the dust from the head of the herd, sporadically at first, and then in a determined fusillade. Greg drew his pistol and spurred his horse forward. The three drag riders had halted their mounts and were staring ahead, wondering at the shooting while uneasiness communicated itself to the cattle. Some turned immediately, as if by instinct, and began to run back towards the distant valley. The drag riders drew their guns, intent on doing their job, and chaos broke over the herd like a thunderstorm.

Greg cocked his Colt and drew a bead on the nearest of the drag riders.

He clenched his teeth and fired. Smoke flew and he screwed up his eyes against it. The rider jerked and twisted, then pulled on his reins convulsively, hauling his mount to a halt. The horse sat back on its haunches, then bucked, and the rider fell out of the saddle. He hit the ground hard and lay still. The horse turned and came back towards Greg, its stirrups flying, and it passed him, running as if bats from hell were pursuing it.

The two men with Greg opened fire. The crash of the shots added to the fear of the cattle. Caught between two fires, they swung away from the drag and began to mill, horns clashing, calves and smaller animals being trampled. The remaining drag riders tried to avoid the cattle, and one twisted in his saddle and fired three shots in Greg's direction. Greg felt the tug of a bullet as it struck the brim of his hat. A second slug burned his left arm between wrist and elbow. Greg threw down on the rustler, only to see him slip sideways out of his saddle to disappear under the flailing hoofs of the steers.

Greg turned his gun on one of the flank riders, who was turning in his direction. They exchanged shots over the backs of the terrified cattle. Dust rose thickly, obscuring vision. The herd was streaming away on the flanks and the rustlers could do nothing about it. They had become embroiled in a sudden and unexpected shoot-out and were hampered by the cattle.

Greg went forward as the herd dispersed, shooting at rustlers as they loomed up, and the two cowboys at his side were keen to kill the rustlers. Cattle bawled and ran. One of the flank riders was unseated by the swelling surge of terrified beef. He pitched to the ground and was trampled; moments later his horse went down and disappeared in the dust. Guns crashed echoingly. Riders fell from their saddles. As Greg rode forward determinedly the cattle moved like a flowing brown river away from the shooting, hoofs pounding, filling the air with a desperate drumming that made the booming shots sound insignificant.

A bunch of riders was coming towards Greg and he held his fire, recognizing Ned Brewster leading them. The rancher had two pistols in his hands and was guiding his horse with his knees, his knotted reins between his teeth. A rustler went down to Brewster's accurate fire, and others fled with the stampeding cattle. Greg traded shots with them as they ran, saw two more rustlers vacate their saddles. Then he paused to reload, and, by the time he was ready to continue the grim fight it was all over.

The cattle were running blindly, coming back together in a brown torrent, running blindly in fear. Greg reckoned that they would not stop inside of five miles. Brewster came towards him, grinning hugely. The shooting had faded away and the cowboys at once turned to look for fallen rustlers, bringing their bodies in and placing them in a line on the hard ground. Greg could see that none of the thieves had escaped. All except one were dead, and the survivor was badly wounded. Two cowboys went ahead to locate the rustlers' chuck wagon and to capture the cook.

Brewster walked along the line of the dead rustlers, looking at each upturned face. He glanced at Greg, who walked by his side.

'Looks like we got them all,' Brewster said. 'Any idea which one is their boss?'

Greg paused beside Chad Sewell, stretched out with two bullets in the centre of his chest. 'I'm not sure,' he said thoughtfully. 'I was watching the goings on at H7 yesterday, and saw a rustler go into the yard and talk to this one.' He stirred Sewell with the toe of his boot. 'I guess it doesn't really matter now. Dead, they are all the same.'

'We'll bury them here,' Brewster declared in a matter of fact tone. 'It's all over now, I guess. I'm glad I got the chance to be in at the kill. I'll have my crew start rounding up the steers and we'll push them back to Antelope Valley. The local ranchers can pick out their brands and take them back to home range.

Greg nodded. Relief was big inside him. He felt as if a black cloud had lifted from his mind. He holstered his pistol and checked his left arm. A red furrow that oozed blood marked his tanned skin. He felt light-headed, hardly able to accept that it was over and he had won. He breathed deeply to rid his nostrils of the smell of gun smoke. His thoughts turned to the coming days as the cares and fears of the past week fell away, and the promise of a peaceful future beckoned him like a shining beacon.

THE END

We do hope that you have enjoyed reading this large print book.

Did you know that all of our titles are available for purchase?

We publish a wide range of high quality large print books including:
Romances, Mysteries, Classics
General Fiction
Non Fiction and Westerns

Special interest titles available in large print are:
The Little Oxford Dictionary
Music Book, Song Book
Hymn Book, Service Book

Also available from us courtesy of Oxford University Press:
Young Readers' Dictionary
(large print edition)
Young Readers' Thesaurus
(large print edition)

For further information or a free brochure, please contact us at:
Ulverscroft Large Print Books Ltd.,
The Green, Bradgate Road, Anstey,
Leicester, LE7 7FU, England.
Tel: (00 44) **0116 236 4325**
Fax: (00 44) **0116 234 0205**

THE VINEGAR PEAK WARS

Hugh Martin

Saddle tramps Cephas Dannehar and Slim Oskin, drifting through the Vinegar Peak country of Arizona Territory, help an old colleague out of trouble, and in doing so get themselves on the wrong side of scheming Nate Sturgis, the self-styled boss of Vinegar Peak. In a lead-peppered struggle between their horse-ranching friends and Sturgis's toughs, bullets are soon flying and fires of destruction lit — all part of the growing pains of a raw western territory shaping its post-Civil War destiny . . .

THE SEARCH FOR THE LONE STAR

I. J. Parnham

It has long been rumoured that the fabulous diamond known as the Lone Star is buried somewhere near the town of Diamond Springs. Many men have died trying to claim it, but when Diamond Springs becomes a ghost town, the men who go there have different aims. Tex Callahan has been paid to complete a mission; Rafferty Horn wants to right a past mistake; George Milligan thinks he knows what has happened to the diamond; and Elias Sutherland wants revenge . . .

LAST MAN IN LAZARUS

Bill Shields

When a town marshal is murdered by five escaping prisoners and his new bride is abducted, the killers think they have avoided the justice they deserve. But the dead man's older brother is Nathan Holly, a feared and relentless US marshal who is more than happy to take up the pursuit. Holly rides north with a Paiute tracker, Tukwa — a man conducting his own quest for vengeance. Both will end their search amidst the winter snows of a mining town called Lazarus . . .